PERHAPS IN POPPY BAY

a novella

Tina Marie Christensen

Perhaps in Poppy Bay

Copyright © 2023 by Tina Marie Christensen

All rights reserved.

ISBN: 979-8398596618

tinamariechristensen.com

For the mermaids.

Chapter 1

"You are perfect," I murmur to the adorable rental cottage just up the driveway.

Wild Rose Cottage is painted crisp white with dark blue trim, and there's a wraparound porch furnished with a few chairs that will be perfect for drinking tea in the early hours, or relaxing in the late evenings after a swim in my mermaid form.

I close the trunk of my car and begin to wheel my suitcase up to the front porch when a lovely, low-timbre voice calls out to me.

"Hi, Lullaby?"

Lifting a hand to shield my eyes from the budding morning sunlight, I see a man wearing a warm smile approaching me from one of the property trails.

I nod in confirmation and the man extends his hand.

"I'm Luke Hamilton, owner of Poppy Bay Cottages."

I shake his hand. "It's a pleasure, Luke."

The front door of a nearby cottage opens, and three people who appear to be in their early twenties exit. They are all holding hands and laughing merrily with one another. One person in their group spots Luke and me, and she gives us an enthusiastic wave.

"I'll meet you at the beach," she tells her group as she trots across the lawn in our direction.

Luke's expression shifts into one of genial affection as the young woman reaches us.

"Hi neighbor!" she says to me cheerfully, rocking back and forth on her bare feet. "I'm Holly."

There's no mistaking that Holly and Luke are related in some way—they both have chestnut brown hair, warm beige skin and blueberry-blue eyes that twinkle with an intriguing combination of mirth and mischief.

"I'm Lullaby."

Holly's blue eyes grow wide and her mouth drops open in astonishment. "Oh my gosh, you're Lullaby of Lullaby's Travels!"

My chin dips in assent, and Holly gives a little squeal of delight.

"I'm a huge fan of your work! I've read five of your travel narratives, and I love how you focus on the magical aspects of the places you visit."

I beam at the genuine tone of Holly's words. "That's fantastic to hear, thank you."

Holly sighs and folds her hands over her heart. "Your work is the reason I signed up for the study abroad program next year with Cal State. Can I please give you a hug?"

"Sure." I extend my arms for the embrace.

Holly gives me a quick squeeze and draws back with her brows lifted. "Are you featuring our California seaside town in your work?"

I give a little shake of my head. "No, my time here is personal. It's a bit of a respite from work, actually."

"Oh, okay." Holly's attention shifts rapidly down to my sandals and back up to my face. "You're so tiny in person; you can't really tell in your photos and videos online."

I offer her a wide grin in response. I can't really fault Holly for the candid observation—at five feet zero inches I'm positively Lilliputian compared to her and Luke, who appear to be just shy of and well over six feet tall, respectively.

"And you look young," Holly continues. "How old are you?"

"Holly," Luke warns. "Please do not interrogate our guest."

"It's okay," I say to Luke. There's a kind of guileless quality to Holly's interest that feels amiable rather than intrusive. Turning to Holly, I answer her question. "I'm thirty."

Holly tilts her head at me. "Are you single? I haven't seen any recent posts of you and Lorenzo traipsing through Italy together, so I'm guessing that romance is *finito*?" There's a barely concealed lilt of hope in her voice.

Luke closes his eyes and pinches the bridge of his nose with his thumb and forefinger, though he doesn't say anything. When his eyes lift to mine, a little tremor of awareness courses throughout my body.

He's curious about the answer as well.

I nod at Holly. "I'm single."

"Excellent." She lays a hand on Luke's shoulder. "This is my brother, Luke. He's thirty-eight years old, sweet most

3

of the time, charming when he wants to be and also, single."

"*Holly.*" A flush of bright color is now tinging Luke's neck, and he looks just about ready to muzzle his sister.

Holly takes a step back from us, her eyes twinkling with innocent mischief. I lower my head to hide the smile spreading across my face.

Clasping her hands demurely in front of her, Holly takes another step back. "That's all from me for now. Have fun you two." With a quick wave and laughter in her eyes, she dashes off towards the beach.

I watch her willowy form disappear over the sand dunes, and turn to see Luke scrubbing a hand down his face.

"I'm sorry about that," he says. "She's only here for a couple more days and then she'll be heading back to university. If she gets to be too much, please let me know and I'll move her to another cottage away from yours. Far away."

I give a soft laugh. "That won't be necessary. She's like a refreshing sea breeze and I'm happy she's my neighbor."

"That's very gracious of you, thank you." He glances at my suitcase. "I'll let you get settled in. Welcome to Poppy Bay, Lullaby." The smooth, low tones of his voice flow over to me like a river of warm honey, and I wave as he walks off to a small trail that runs behind my building and into a cluster of pine trees.

He disappears into the trees, and I wheel my suitcase up to the charming little cottage that will be my home for the next month.

I unlock the front door and pull my suitcase through the narrow entryway that leads to a spacious living room, dining room and open kitchen. The décor is coastal chic, with soft-hued beach paintings on the wall, sage green furniture and sheer ivory curtains.

Everything feels fresh and airy in here, and I smile as I make my way to the bedroom at the end of the short hallway. The bed is covered in classic white bedding, there are pastel seashell prints on the wall and white curtains billowing in the breeze flowing through the open window.

I unpack my suitcase then head to the kitchen to get a glass of water, and take it outside to the front porch.

Standing at the railing, I inhale deeply. The air smells of brine and pine—it's an exquisite and rejuvenating combination. From here, I have a view of the sand dunes, with the expansive bay just beyond them. The ocean waves flowing into the bay sound like an enchanting song, and I close my eyes to enjoy the mellifluous melody.

Even if I weren't a mermaid, I think I would still be intrinsically drawn to the sea. There's such a feeling of wild freedom in it for me, and I can't imagine ever not feeling the lure of that great blue realm.

I've met many humans in my travels who possess an affinity with the sea, but I often wish I had other merpeople to share the deep connection with.

For the past decade, I have searched most of the world looking for other merfolk, whether on land or within the ocean's depths. And while I've encountered many terrific souls who have mermaid-like qualities, I have yet to meet an actual merperson like myself.

My quest to find other merfolk has all been done under the guise of Lullaby's Travels, my beloved travel lifestyle business. And even though I've experienced great wonder and beauty on my adventures, I have recently begun to feel a bone-deep exhaustion with my merfolk search. Which is what brought me here, to Poppy Bay on California's Sonoma Coast.

With ten years of fruitless searching under my belt, there's a part of me that is just about ready to give up altogether. So I want to use the next month to relax and recharge, and to figure out a new game plan for my merfamily search. I do intend to explore the local waters though, just in case there is someone of my kind here.

I open my eyes and stare out at the rippling water of the bay. Even with the flicker of hope that burns bright within my heart and inspires me to keep seeking, at times it feels like I may very well be the last mermaid on Earth.

Chapter 2

"Hi Lullaby!"

A cheery voice stirs me from my mermaid extinction thoughts, and I blink a few times to see Holly approaching the cottage.

"I just popped by to invite you to swim with us," she says with a bright smile. "Will you come?"

"In the bay?" I ask with a slight frown. "I thought Northern California beaches were a little too cold and rough for swimming?"

Even though it's summer, there's a chill to the air that tells me the water will also have a frosty bite to it. Not to mention the strong currents typical of the beaches this far north on the Pacific Coast. When I'm in mermaid form, my body can tolerate wide variances in water temperature and conditions, but in human form I generally prefer more temperate swims.

Holly hops up the stairs to the porch, still barefoot just as she was earlier in the morning. "We're not swimming in the bay; we're swimming at Luke's house. There is a swimming beach at the south end of the bay, where the waves and temperature are milder, but Luke's pool is heated so we usually just swim there." She points to the pine trees behind my cottage. "He lives just on the other side of the trees."

A quiver of excitement runs through me at the thought of seeing Luke again so soon. "I'll join you; I just need to grab a swimsuit. You're welcome to come inside while I change."

Holly follows me into the cottage and waits in the living room while I put on a deep burgundy one-piece in the bedroom. I throw my heather gray t-shirt and jean shorts back on over the bathing suit, and we leave the cottage for the trail that curves into the pine trees.

We reach Luke's house, which is exquisitely designed and boasts an unobscured view of the bay. In stark contrast to the charm and quaintness of the cottages, the house is all clean lines, sleek stone and walls of wide windows.

Holly guides me to the backyard, which is concealed by a tall slatted fence. She opens a gate in the fence and we step into a lush oasis that is surreal in its beauty.

Rows of low shrubs with little yellow flowers flank the concrete walkway, there's a pretty pergola with a wide swing that could also serve as a bed, and an elegant pool with cascading waterfalls flowing serenely into it.

Luke is standing at the far end of the pool in front of a large grill, while the two people I saw earlier with Holly are splashing about in the water.

"I brought a friend," Holly declares as we reach Luke.

Luke's lips melt into a warm smile, and I reflect his smile in greeting. He's barefoot in a white tee and ice blue shorts; his brown hair is glimmering with bronze highlights in the bright sunlight.

"I'm so glad you came, Lullaby," he says. "There's an abundance of food here, and we could really use your help eating it."

Holly points to the two people in the pool. "That is my boyfriend, Min-Jun. And my girlfriend, Kendra."

Min-Jun is an attractive young man with bleached blond hair and kind sable eyes. With a voluptuous figure and long copper hair, Kendra looks very much like a goddess of sensual beauty.

They both wave at me in greeting, and I wave back. Holly tugs off her shirt and shorts, leaves them on the ground next to us and dives into the pool. Min-Jun floats a lime green pool noodle her way; she drapes her arms over it and rests her cheek on the foam, closing her eyes to the sunshine.

I turn to Luke, studying his profile as he flips a chicken breast on the grill. His jawline is like the rugged outline of a mountain range—sharp, hard, powerful. Something I could spend the whole day quietly admiring.

Luke's attention shifts to me, and he gestures to a small stainless steel refrigerator under the pergola. "There are beverages in the cooler, if you'd like a drink?"

I walk to the fridge and take out a bottle of sparkling water. Slipping off my sandals, I sip the water while watching Luke work at the grill. There are a few pieces of chicken on it and a plethora of vegetables: summer squashes, sweet potatoes, corn and portobello mushrooms. He adjusts a few of the chicken pieces and sets the tongs aside.

He grabs new tongs to flip the vegetables. "I looked up some of your work; Lullaby's Travels is impressive."

Lambent pleasure flows through me at his interest in my career. "Thank you. I love my work, though I am enjoying this break from it. Poppy Bay is so picturesque though, the writer in me can't help but internally narrate all of the beauty of it."

"Where's your home base? Or are you totally nomadic?"

"I have an apartment in Seattle." I take a sip of water. "Though with all of my traveling, I actually spend very little time there."

Luke nods in understanding and I glance at the pool, where Holly, Min-Jun and Kendra are now lounging on single-person floats. The three of them are clasping hands, occasionally drawing each other near to exchange soft kisses.

"They're cute together," I comment.

Luke gives the group a glimpse before shifting his focus back to the grill. "Yeah, it's cute until I have to pick up the pieces of Holly's shattered heart."

I'm getting the feeling that Luke is a sort of father figure in Holly's life, and I can't help but wonder about their parents. There's probably a story there, but I refrain from asking about it.

"You don't believe in love?" I ask instead.

Luke turns to me, his lips pressed into a small smile. "I believe in love. But they're only twenty years old — they have so much growing up to do still, and I don't really see how that will work out for them in the long run."

I tilt my head at him. "Maybe it doesn't matter if it lasts. Maybe it's more important that they're happy now."

His small smile widens into a full grin. "Fair point."

The sliding glass door leading into the house opens, and a woman steps out to the backyard.

"I smell food," she declares. She's wearing a law enforcement uniform that is somehow made adorable by her very round belly.

Luke's eyes alight with joy. "You made it. Lullaby, this is my sister Christine. She's the sheriff of Poppy Bay."

Christine waves as she ambles over to our side of the pool. She has the same brown hair and blueberry-blue eyes as Luke and Holly. She's substantially shorter than either of them, though she appears to be the middle sibling.

"Chris, come swim with us!" Holly calls out from the water.

Christine peers down at her uniform and back up at Holly. "Not now, kiddo. I have to get back to work."

Luke points to the food on the grill. "To go then?"

Christine smiles wide. "Yes please."

"I'll grab some containers," Luke says. "Be right back."

He enters the house, and Christine turns to me.

"How do you know Luke?" she asks without preamble. While Holly seems to be carefree, and Luke nurturing, I can tell straight away that Christine is the more serious of the three siblings. Her blue eyes have a piercing astuteness to them that seem to absorb every detail in her line of sight, which I suppose is a beneficial quality to have in her line of work.

11

I motion to the fence, in the direction of Poppy Bay Cottages. "I'm renting a cottage from Luke; Holly is my neighbor and she invited me to swim here."

Christine's chin dips in a curt nod. "Lullaby is an interesting name—what's the story behind it?"

I shrug my shoulders. "It's nothing special. When my parents adopted me as an infant, they said I was very serene and smiled the whole ride home. They said I seemed like a darling lullaby to them."

Christine cradles her belly affectionately, her sharp eyes softening into maternal devotion. "That's sweet. Maybe baby number three here will have a similar naming story."

Luke emerges from the house with several containers, and he packs his sister a massive meal of vegetables, chicken and a few of the salad and side items from the picnic table under the pergola. He tucks everything into a tote bag for her, and she kisses his cheek before turning to me.

"Nice to meet you, Lullaby." She shifts to Holly and says, "I'll see you later tonight with Omari and the kids."

"See you then," Holly replies with a wave.

Christine leaves, and Luke beckons to the group in the pool.

"Everything's ready," he says. "Come eat."

Holly, Kendra and Min-Jun exit the pool, grab towels and walk over to the picnic table while Luke moves all of the chicken and vegetables to serving platters. He places the platters on the picnic table next to the salads and side dishes, and we all pile our plates with food.

The three college students chat happily about school while we eat, which allows me to simply relax and be

12

present with their vibrant energy. Luke asks them a few questions about school, though he seems to mainly enjoy just listening to them share funny stories about college life.

Occasionally he studies me, as though checking on my comfort levels, and I always respond with a beatific smile.

We finish eating lunch and relax under the pergola for a spell, then Holly, Kendra and Min-Jun return to the pool.

"Come in the water with us!" Holly calls out to Luke and me.

In response to Holly's summons, Luke stands and strips off his shirt. He's long and lean like a professional baseball player, with well-defined muscles that are glimmering gorgeous in the sunshine.

He holds his hand out to me. "Want to go for a swim?"

If he only knew how much that simple question brings me joy. As a mermaid, anyone asking me to spend time in water gains an immediate and cozy spot in my heart. Holly's already there for having invited me initially, and now Luke.

I stand and remove my t-shirt and shorts. When I look up at Luke, I notice that his pupils have widened into black saucers, which I'm fairly certain has nothing to do with how the burgundy swimsuit complements my olive skin and chin-length, wavy black hair.

I rather think it has something to do with the round curves of my hips and weighty fullness of my breasts. A former Spanish lover once asked me how I fit so much decadent flesh into such a small package, and I'd say that description of my body is fairly accurate. Petite with lush curves that I'm aware have turned many heads throughout my adult life.

Luke's extended hand drops to his side, and I just can't help myself—I saunter past him with my seductive mermaid allure turned on full blast, and dive sleekly into the pool.

Chapter 3

When I surface from the pool water, I shine an angelic smile Luke's way and ask, "Are you coming?"

With a small shake of his head, Luke mutters something under his breath that sounds like, "I'm in trouble." He takes a couple of steps and dives over my head into the water.

We all splash about and play pool games, which is so much fun the time just flies by. But when the afternoon sun starts to dip low into the horizon, a great wave of fatigue washes over me.

My full day of traveling and socializing has finally caught up with me, and with weariness now permeating my bones I exit the pool.

I take a towel from a poolside cabinet, wrap it around my chest and walk to the wide swing under the pergola. I take a seat and rock back and forth, with the tranquil movement causing my eyelids to droop with exhaustion.

Luke leaves the pool and grabs a towel, wrapping it around his waist and sitting down next to me.

"Are you okay?" he asks, his eyes creased in concern.

I place my palms onto my eyes, attempting to rub away some of the fatigue. "Yes, I think the travel and full day has just caught up with me. I should probably head back to the cottage." But the thought of even that small trek feels like too much effort at the moment, and my body melts down into the expansive cushion.

Luke eyes my sinking body with a press of his lips, while his feet take over pushing the swing in a placid, soothing rhythm. "You can take a nap here," he offers.

As someone who travels for a living, I'm well aware of the personal safety issues this type of scenario may present. Through the years however, I've finely honed my intuition about safe places and people in general, and the only thing I can detect with Luke at this time is genuine consideration for my comfort and well-being.

I curl up on my side, trying and failing to stifle a yawn. "Are you sure? Napping here on my first day of meeting you would be really poor guest etiquette."

"I don't give a damn about any of that," Luke says softly. "Just be comfortable here."

I cast a sleepy smile up at him. "Holly was right about you—you are sweet."

Planting his hands on his knees, he stands from the swing, though I wouldn't mind at all if he curled his long body around mine and dozed with me.

Luke regards me with a wry smile. "I'm pretty sure she also said I'm charming."

A little laugh departs my throat, and before my eyelids drift closed I murmur, "That too."

* * *

16

"Lullaby?" A deep voice rouses me from my nap.

I open my eyes to see Luke sitting on the swing with me. With a bleary gaze, I peer up at the sky through the slats of the pergola. The sun has already set, and stars are just starting to appear in the inky darkness above.

I sit up and rub my eyes. "How long was I asleep for?" There's a light blanket covering me, and a cozy fire burning in the nearby fire pit.

"A couple of hours. You looked deep asleep, and we didn't want to wake you. You probably needed it after such a long day."

"Probably." I lift my arms high above my head to give my back a long stretch. "Well, I'm sorry for being such poor company, though I do appreciate you letting me rest."

"There's nothing to apologize for." Luke gestures to the sliding glass door, where Holly, Min-Jun and Kendra are sitting inside the living room on a wide sofa. "Christine and her husband Omari will be here soon with their two children. We're going to order pizza and watch movies — you're welcome to stay and join us."

I consider the invitation for a moment. It's only been one day and it feels like Luke and Holly have already enfolded me into their family.

"Are you this kind and welcoming to all of your guests?" I ask, peering up at Luke's profile.

He turns to me with a smile. "Yes, I am. Though I don't generally invite them to participate in our personal family activities."

Gratification flows through me at his response, and I observe him candidly for a few moments. The thought of

17

spending more time doing fun family stuff with Luke and Holly is very tempting, but the ocean is calling me to swim, in my mermaid form.

Even from Luke's backyard, I can hear waves rolling up to the shore, each one a summons for me to go to the water. I close my eyes briefly, inhaling the sharp briny air and allowing the magic of the ocean to seep into my skin.

With another long stretch, I stand from the swing. "I would love to join you another time; tonight I think I'm just going to head back to the cottage."

"Okay." Luke stands as well. "Do you want to say goodbye to everyone?"

"Yes, that would be great."

Luke leads me to the sliding glass door and opens it; I pop my head in and say goodnight to the group, and apologize for my slumberous absence. The three of them wave off the apology with cheerful smiles, and I follow Luke back out to the pool area.

"Is it okay if I escort you home?" he asks, navigating us through the backyard and to the gate that leads to the cottage trail.

"That would be nice." I pause to place a hand on his forearm. "And thank you for your hospitality—I really do appreciate it."

Luke looks down at where my hand is on his arm. The connection point between us is hot, flowing with kinetic energy.

His free hand lifts to trace small lines across the top of my wrist; the light strokes hasten my breath, while liquid heat begins to pool in my lower abdomen.

It's a wonder to me how a simple touch can feel so excruciatingly good.

"I'm happy you're here," he says, still tracing lines along my wrist.

A car pulls up in Luke's driveway, and Christine and her family emerge from it. Before they have a chance to see us, Luke links his fingers in mine and gently guides me along the trail that leads to Wild Rose Cottage.

The path is well-lit with ground lights, and the air feels clean and crisp. When we reach my driveway, Luke bids me goodnight, and he waits until I'm safely inside before turning back onto the trail.

* * *

It's after midnight when I leave the cottage again.

This time, I take the trail that leads to the sand dunes and the bay. I walk along the dark beach, enjoying the brisk breeze rippling through the night, and the nourishing sound of the waves.

I walk past Luke's house and to the north end of the bay, where large boulders create a rough path jutting out to sea. The rock formations will offer a nice concealment for my shift and swim.

There are several seagulls sleeping on the large rocks, and I remove my clothes with smooth and hushed movements, careful not to wake them. I'm still wearing my bathing suit from earlier in the day, but I strip that off as well. I wrap my clothes in a towel and tuck everything into a boulder's shielded nook.

I step quickly into the water, and the frigid cold of the bay strikes me immediately. As soon as the water reaches my knees I begin to shift into my mermaid form.

Several gill slits open on both sides of my neck, and my skin takes on a minty green hue. My vision sharpens remarkably, with the nightscape taking on new textures, depth and colors, and the transformation is complete when my legs merge and curve into a long tail that shimmers with purple, blue, silver and green scales.

The shift into my mermaid form eases any discomfort from the bay's temperature, and my body now feels as though I'm swimming in the tropical waters of the Caribbean: sultry, warm and silky.

I swim within the bay, taking my time and turning on my back like a sea otter. My luminescent tail swishes smoothly as I float by sleeping harbor seals whose heads are bobbing just above the surface of the water.

The night sky is filled with glittering stars and wisps of clouds that are passing over the bright moon like gossamer ghosts on a celestial journey. Fanning my arms out, I relax into the night and into the mystical beauty of the sea.

Deciding to do some underwater exploring of the bay, I dive down to the seafloor, where I find a group of elegant leopard sharks feeding on the sandy bottom. Their silvery-bronze skin and dark spots are ethereal in the nightscape, and I admire their sleek forms for a few moments before winding my way through a dense kelp forest and swimming beyond the bounds of the bay.

Once in the depths of the ocean, I swim around to get my bearings of the area and then send out my mermaid call, which is a series of crystalline notes that expand out for thousands of miles, similar to a whale song.

The high frequency notes vibrate through the water and I listen, doing my best to temper the hope that inevitably flares in my chest each time I send out the call.

When there's no response, I send out the call again.

This time I do receive a deep, pulsed response from a nearby pod of humpback whales.

Though the return whale call is soothing and peaceful, it is not what I was hoping for.

In all of the years I've been sending out my call, I've yet to receive a response from another merperson. I suppose at this point the lack of response shouldn't affect me so intensely, but it still does.

Each time I receive a return call from a being other than a merperson—or nothing at all—my heart feels a little heavy, and a little sad.

Tonight is no exception, and I find myself feeling a sense of loss that is somehow both intangible and deeply visceral.

With a weary underwater sigh, I turn and swim back towards the bay.

Chapter 4

Shifting into my human form as I approach the shore, I jog to where my clothes and towel are stashed. I tug the towel from the rock cubby, dry myself off in brisk strokes and get dressed.

As I make my way along the night-shrouded beach, I spot another person walking in my direction. Though the darkness has cast everything in deep shadows, the flutter of awareness low in my belly tells me exactly who it is.

"Lullaby?" Luke asks with great surprise lacing his voice.

I wave in greeting. "Hi."

He assesses the towel draped over my shoulder and my damp hair with a furrow of his brow. "Did you go swimming?"

"Not quite," I hedge. "I was sitting on the towel near the shore when a wave came up too close and got me wet."

One corner of Luke's mouth twists in a dubious expression, but he doesn't comment on it further.

"You're up late," I say to change the subject. "Do you normally enjoy after-midnight walks along the beach?"

Luke nods. "Most nights, yes. I like the peaceful lull of activity at this hour."

"This is my favorite time to be out here," I say with a smile.

Luke hesitates for a moment, and I can tell he wants to say something.

"What is it?" I ask.

His lips press between his teeth as he peers down at me. "I know that you're an adult who travels for a living, and I'm sure you can take care of yourself."

"But..." I prompt gently.

"But this is a tourist town, and based on some of the things Christine has shared with me, I wouldn't bank on the wholesome intentions of every one of our visitors. Especially with someone like you, walking alone on a beach at night."

My head tilts in question, though I'm very well aware of where he's headed with this conversation. "Someone like me?"

Luke hesitates again, and my sense is that he's attempting to phrase his next statement with as much pragmatism as possible. He holds his hand out near my head, which barely reaches his chest. "Someone with your diminutive stature," he finally says.

I give a little laugh. "I may be short, but I know how to be safe in new and unfamiliar environments. So you don't have to worry about me."

He exhales a deep breath. "Okay, good."

I give his shoulder a playful push. "This must be how Holly and Christine feel being your younger sisters."

Clamping the back of his neck with his hand, he peers out at the inky water. "I can assure you that I have no desire to be a brother to you." His eyes shift to mine, and even in the darkness I can see the incandescent implication burning in them.

Heat travels from my chest down to my inner thighs at his sustained regard, and I clasp my lower lip with my teeth, trying to quell the desire swelling within me.

Luke's eyes crinkle into a knowing smile, and he thumbs back towards his house. "I was just heading back to my place — do you want to come over for a bit and warm up by the fire?"

"Yes," I respond instantly, though we both know I can start a cozy gas fire in my cottage hearth with the simple flick of a switch.

"Great." Turning on his bare heel in the sand, he holds out his arm to me and we make our way back to his house.

When we arrive, he immediately lights a fire in the living room fireplace, and offers to make chamomile tea.

He starts the tea preparation in the kitchen, while I admire the interior of his home. I only got a brief peek at it when I was saying goodbye to Holly and crew earlier in the day.

The large sofa and loveseat are dark brown with blue throw pillows. The prints on the wall are abstracts with clean strokes of beige paint, giving the overall feel of the space a subtle and almost subdued feel, though something tells me the understated look is intentional.

One entire wall of the living room is made up of tall windows, and I imagine that during the daytime, the expansive view of the bay outside is what takes center stage in terms of the home's visual features.

The open plan shifts seamlessly into the sleek and modern kitchen with an island that's as large as my entire kitchen in Seattle. There's no formal dining area; instead a collection of cushioned stools flank the island and appear to serve as the dining table.

A hallway extends just beyond the kitchen, and it likely leads to the bedrooms and bathrooms of the single level house. The first door in the hallway is slightly open, and inside appears to be a home gym with two low shelves of free weights and other equipment. Based on what I've seen of Luke's body, I'd say he uses the room with dedicated regularity, which is a great contrast to the personal aversion I feel towards gym equipment. I prefer to exercise outdoors—swimming, hiking around lakes or jogging along the beach. Anything with fresh air and preferably, water.

I walk over to the hearth to warm my hands by the fire, and notice several photos on the mantel of what appear to be Luke's parents. The photos look dated, judging by the infant they are holding, and how young Luke and Christine appear to be in them.

"Are these your parents?" I ask Luke, pointing to the photos.

Carrying a tea mug over to me and setting one for himself on the coffee table, he nods. "Our parents both released their bodies when Holly was only two years old. I was twenty and Christine was sixteen. It was a car accident while they were on vacation in Oregon."

I sink onto the sofa, my heart wrenching for Luke and his sisters. "Oh heck, I'm so sorry. That must have been incredibly difficult for all of you."

Luke takes a seat next to me and picks up his mug. "It was difficult at the time, but we got through it. I became Holly and Christine's legal guardian after the accident; we didn't have any other family. In some ways I see their passing as a blessing—it brought Holly, Christine and me together in a way we never would have been with our parents still around."

"I think I understand. My parents adopted me as an infant, and my adoptive mother transitioned when I was ten; she had a fatal allergic reaction to an insect bite. Without Mom around, Dad and I developed a deep bond that we probably wouldn't have had otherwise."

He nods. "Yeah, you get it. I know many people would think it's callous to say their parents' death was a blessing, especially for ones like ours who were very loving and caring."

I take a sip of my tea and smile. "So you're essentially Holly and Christine's father...things make a lot more sense now."

Luke peers at me over his cup. "How so?"

"Your nurturing and protective qualities. Would you still be that way if your parents had survived?"

Luke laughs, deeply and heartily. "As their older brother, I'm sure I would still be protective. But you're right, probably not to the degree I am now."

I shift on the sofa and study the family photos on the mantel. "How do you feel about Christine being the sheriff

26

of Poppy Bay? I imagine the crime here is less severe than other areas of the state, but still. It's dangerous work."

He leans back on the sofa with a grunt. "That was really hard for me to accept initially, but I had to let it go. Christine loves serving in that way, and she's very good at her job." His lips melt into a smile. "Even now while she's preparing for baby number three to enter her life."

"Do you want to have children of your own? Or is that too personal of a question?"

"It's not too personal. And no, I don't want children of my own—I actually had a vasectomy two years ago. I was in a long-term relationship at the time, and I knew that my desire to not father children wasn't going to change." He takes a drink of his tea. "Holly and Christine have been more than enough parenting for me. I do enjoy being a doting uncle to Christine's kids though, I just don't want any of my own. How about you? Do you want children?"

I shake my head. "I knew very early on in life that I didn't want children; there are too many things I want to experience that don't involve me being a mother." Even if I am the last of my kind, I still have less than zero desire to procreate with another being, human or otherwise.

Luke gives me an appraising look. "It's nice to have that kind of clarity about life."

I tilt my head at him. "I like that we've only just met, and yet we can talk about all of these personal things comfortably."

He shrugs and casts me a half-smile. "I'm not big on small talk."

I lift my hand to tick points off on my fingers. "You're not big on small talk, you don't want children, and you love

27

swimming and nighttime walks along the beach. Luke Hamilton, I just may have to marry you."

Luke's eyes darken, and he regards me for a few silent moments that stretch into endless minutes.

"Did I really say that aloud?" I stammer quickly. "I think I'm getting delirious with fatigue—it's been a long day."

Still, he doesn't speak. I swallow thickly, and finally he bursts out laughing. It's loud and deep and wonderful, and I laugh right along with him, elated tears touching the corners of my eyes.

Our laughter subsides, and with a swift wipe of my eyes, I set the mug on the coffee table and stand. "I should get back to the cottage, otherwise I may fall asleep here again."

Luke stands and says in his low-timbre voice, "That wouldn't be a problem for me."

His candid statement shifts the mood from playful to provocative, and I look up into his blueberry-blue eyes, exhaling a quiet breath. Every sensual siren cell in my body is telling me to lift up and press my mouth onto his lips. I'm only here for one month though, and maybe I'm being presumptuous, but Luke doesn't really strike me as a 'tourist fling' type of local.

"Can I walk you home?" he asks, still holding my gaze.

"Yes," I breathe, forcing my eyes away from the depths of his.

We walk to the door and exit the house, getting onto the trail that leads to the cottage. Luke says goodnight at my driveway, and again watches until I'm safely inside before turning back onto the trail.

"Damn," I whisper as I peek out a window, watching him disappear into the shadows of the trees.

I'm accustomed to having a healthy measure of self-mastery in my romantic endeavors, and most if not all of them have been without any real attachment or complications. But with Luke all of that just seems to crumble at my feet. Being with him feels like falling headlong into a big scary well of unknown.

I step away from the window with a sigh. As long as I'm actively searching for my merfamily, I know that any potential lover will only get fragments of me—never my whole self. And someone like Luke who is all goodness and guileless heart...he deserves *everything*. Which is far more than what I can give anyone at this juncture of my life.

Resolving to steer clear of any romantic entanglements with him, I strip off my clothes and enter the bathroom. I start the shower and step into the flow of hot water, allowing it to wash away any residue from my sea swim. After soaping off the last bits of salt, I close my eyes and relax under the sensuous spray.

The rivulets of water trailing down my skin feel like hot kisses on my body—Luke's hot kisses specifically. My fingers reach up to graze my collarbone, and they follow the trail of water down my breasts and to the damp heat between my thighs.

I may be determined to avoid physical intimacy with Luke, but that won't stop me from using my imagination to enjoy his magnificent body.

I caress myself with soft strokes, imagining Luke and me in the shower together. A vivid image of my legs wrapped around his waist as he's buried deep within me

29

flashes into my mind, and my breath quickens at the lucid scene. With a low moan, I slide two fingers into my body, while my other hand presses into my folds to rub my pulsing nub.

The mental image of Luke and me shifts to only Luke, wearing the clothes he was wearing tonight. His eyes are closed and he's stroking his hard length, with my name burning on his lips.

The vision is so vivid and erotic that it brings me to an immediate climax.

"Luke," I gasp, clutching the tile wall and breathing through the whole-body shudders. "*Luke.*"

Chapter 5

The next morning I awaken early, feeling well-rested and ravenous.

I put on a white tee, violet leggings and sandals, and decide to head into town to do some exploring. And to acquire some food to appease my rumbling stomach.

There are several walking trails that lead to Main Street, but I take my car so I don't end up having to carry a surplus of shopping bags back to the cottage.

Main Street is bustling with pedestrian activity even at this early hour. The thoroughfare is lined with hanging baskets filled with colorful flowers, and vintage lampposts that likely create a nice atmosphere at night.

I park at one of the public lots, and the first thing I see when I exit my car is a sign for Sunny Sea Bistro. The sign includes a lovely image of a mermaid sunning herself on large rocks.

Deciding that Sunny Sea Bistro is where I must dine today, I walk to the establishment and check the menu that is posted on the wall outside the entrance. It appears that they only serve breakfast, brunch and lunch, and my mouth waters just reading the sumptuous options.

I enter the bistro, admiring the whimsical teal and gold décor speckled throughout the modest space. There's an area on one side of the room that has several dining tables, and a long counter on the other side with bar stools. Wide windows overlooking the bay comprise the whole back wall.

The tables are all full with customers, though there are a couple of empty stools at the dining counter.

I take a seat at the counter, and review the breakfast menu while opening my mermaid intuition to see if there are any actual merfolk within this establishment.

Just as my mermaid call is an underwater form of communication, my mermaid intuition is a land-based way for me to detect other merpeople near me. Even though I haven't ever pinged with another merperson while using it, it's still an ability I naturally know how to use, presumably in the same way bats and dolphins know how to use echolocation.

When I don't sense any other merpeople within the bistro, I tease open my intuition to encompass Main Street, and expand it out farther to the whole town.

I can detect no other mer-life in the area though, so I close my intuition and continue perusing the menu.

A man in his middle years approaches from behind the dining counter and offers me a bright smile. He's wearing a white Sunny Sea apron, has hazel-green eyes and perfectly sculpted eyebrows. Two pretty pearl barrettes are fastened into his short, silver-white hair.

"Welcome to Sunny Sea Bistro; I am Sunny," he says with a charming sort of innocence that I take an immediate liking to. "Are you all set to order, or would you like more time to review the menu?"

I close the menu with a smile. "I'm ready." I order the chicken apple sausage scramble with herb potatoes, and a cup of peppermint tea.

Sunny enters my order into a sleek tablet and tucks it into his apron pocket. "What's your name, dear?" he asks while preparing my tea at the beverage station.

"I'm Lullaby."

He sets the tea mug on the counter. "Where are you visiting from, Lullaby?"

Everywhere and nowhere. "Seattle," I say aloud. "How did you know I'm not local?" Poppy Bay is a smaller California town, but it doesn't seem so small that everyone would know everyone here, at least I wouldn't think so.

Sunny motions his hands as though outlining my head and shoulders. "You have the spirit of a wanderer."

Another man walks behind the counter, carrying several tote bags overflowing with fresh produce and loaves of bread.

"My love," he says, planting a kiss on Sunny's cheek. The man has deep bronze skin, a shaved head, and long black lashes framing golden brown eyes.

Sunny turns to me with a smile. "Alejandro, this is Lullaby. She's visiting from Seattle."

"Oh nice," Alejandro says. "Welcome to Poppy Bay. Where are you staying?"

Both Alejandro and Sunny are emanating genuine friendliness, so my sense is that it's safe to divulge this

33

information to them, though I have on a number of occasions hedged the question while traveling.

"I'm staying at Poppy Bay Cottages."

Sunny clasps his hands in front of his chest, almost like a cheerleader who's about to start a cheer. "That's Luke's place." He runs his hand down Alejandro's arm. "Luke and Alejandro have been best friends since elementary school."

Alejandro nods. "Luke's a good guy." Lifting the grocery bags onto his shoulder, he says, "I'm going to take these back to the kitchen. Nice to meet you, Lullaby."

I wave as Alejandro crosses the threshold to the kitchen, and Sunny asks me, "How long are you here for?"

A server emerges from the kitchen and sets an enormous breakfast platter in front of me. "I'm here for one month."

"Great," Sunny says. "You'll be here for the meteor shower—it's a glorious display of celestial beauty. Enjoy your meal, dear."

I nod and dig into the hearty breakfast. I remember reading about the annual meteor shower during my initial Poppy Bay research. Apparently the cosmic event is a big draw for the town, with stargazers coming from around the country to enjoy the dark skies and unobstructed coastal views.

Sunny chats with the other counter guests—occasionally checking in with me—while I savor every delicious bite of the scrambled eggs, sausage and herby potatoes.

I finish my meal, and just as I'm paying the check, Holly, Min-Jun and Kendra enter the bistro and walk up to the counter.

34

"Lullaby, hi!" Holly says when she sees me. She wraps me in a brief hug and steps back. "We're just picking up a to-go order; what are you up to today?"

I stand from the counter and tuck the meal receipt into my purse. "I'm just doing a bit of exploring today, and some grocery shopping as well." I learned very early on in my travels that while dining out for each meal feels adventurous initially, it's not long before I'm craving fresh vegetables and simple proteins—without all of the butter and sauces and flair that generally come with restaurant meals.

Holly's eyes light up. "You should go to Main Street Market; they have a ton of locally grown produce."

"Great, thank you for the suggestion. I'll stop by there at some point today."

Holly shakes her head. "You should go there, like, now."

I tilt my head in question at her, but she doesn't elaborate. "Okay, I'll go there now."

With a wave, I leave the bistro and walk a few doors down to Main Street Market. The large brick building smells heavenly inside, like freshly baked chocolate chip cookies drizzled with warm caramel. Almost half of the spacious interior is dedicated to self-serve and prepared food options.

I grab a basket and wind my way through the dense mass of other shoppers, stopping first in the produce section. Something in my intuition pings, though it's not for other merpeople. Curious about the trace of heightened awareness now rippling throughout my body, I survey the produce area until I spot Luke, who is adding organic

35

avocados to his basket. Casual in a hunter green t-shirt and jeans, he's seemingly unaware of the absurd number of shoppers—in a variety of genders—who are sending flirtatious looks of appreciation his way.

With a low chuckle, I mutter, "Holly." Now I know why she wanted me to come here immediately. I stride past the rows of fresh fruits and vegetables to where Luke is standing. "Hello, Luke."

Luke turns and peers down at me, his eyes lighting up with pleasure. "Lullaby, it's great to see you. How was your first night at the cottage?"

Thoughts about my first night in the cottage shower rise up in my mind, especially the very clear vision of Luke pleasuring himself with my name on his lips. Liquid heat pools in my lower abdomen, and I clear my throat, mainly in an attempt to clear my mind of erotic thoughts while standing in a brightly lit grocery store.

"It was really nice," I say. "I slept like a baby koala."

One corner of his mouth quirks in a half-smile. "That's very specific; do baby koalas sleep deeply?"

A little laugh escapes me. "I don't know for certain, but I would imagine so, considering they get to be all snuggled up in their mama's pouches."

Luke chuckles and gestures to my basket. "Are you stocking up for the cottage?"

I hold up my empty basket. "I am, though I'm just getting started." Eyeing his full basket, I ask, "Are you making anything special today?"

"It's mostly sandwich stuff for my wildflower picnic. You should come to the picnic—unless you have other plans for the day?"

My lips twist in consideration. "That sounds tempting, but I don't want to impose on anyone."

"No imposition. It's just me, and I'm inviting you."

My head tilts in surprise. "You're going on a wildflower picnic by yourself?" The visual of Luke picnicking by himself in a field of summer wildflowers is just too much — the sheer sweetness of it almost has my knees buckling in a swoon.

Luke grins. "I like the flowers, and I know a nice spot away from all of the tourists. So what do you say, join me for the day?"

My heart gives a little squeeze; the more I learn about Luke the more mythical he seems, like a majestic unicorn in an enchanted forest. And this is coming from someone who is an actual mermaid so, there's that.

"It sounds like fun," I say. "I'd love to go. I'm just going to finish shopping, and then can I meet you at your house in about an hour?"

Luke's smile is like pure sunshine — all joy and golden light. "That's perfect."

We exchange phone numbers in case anything comes up that prevents me from meeting the timeframe, and I spend the rest of my shopping trip in giddy anticipation of picnicking in a field of wildflowers with Luke.

Chapter 6

Luke drives us north along the coast for about twenty minutes, then he turns onto a narrow road that ends in a gravel parking area.

There are only a couple of vacant spaces left, with cars and several camper vans already occupying most of the lot.

Luke parks his truck, and as soon as I step outside I inhale the clean ocean air, glad to have brought a warm hoodie with me to abate some of the coastal chill in this area.

The parking lot is flanked with lush meadows filled with green grass and vibrant wildflowers, while just across the main road the wild and wonderful Pacific Ocean expands out into the horizon.

There are several wooden plank paths running over the meadows, with dog-walkers and hikers enjoying the view, and many visitors taking photos of the stunning scenery.

"It's beautiful here," I say with a gratified sigh. "I love it."

Luke smiles at me, then grabs a folded blanket and backpack from the rear seat of his truck before closing the door. He points to a forest of redwood trees just beyond the meadows. "We're going that way."

We take a wooden walkway that leads into the majestic trees. Once in the forest, the path shifts into a standard natural terrain trail. It's tranquil in the trees, with less people and fainter sounds of the ocean.

We walk along the path until Luke draws apart a dense patch of ferns that is shielding a very narrow trail.

"Is this the way to the secret spot?" I ask in a whisper so none of the other visitors can hear me.

He chuckles. "Yes."

The trail is scarcely wide enough for my sandals, and we have to gently push some plants aside to trek it, but Luke continues on the narrow path with confidence and ease.

The trail steadily inclines until we reach a sequestered meadow that has a perfect and unobstructed view of the sea. There's a small stream flowing through the meadow, down the hill and into the redwoods.

Luke guides me to a flat patch of grass that looks perfect for sitting.

"We're here," he announces, unfolding the blanket and laying it on the ground, then setting the backpack on top of the blanket.

"Wow," I breathe as I turn in a circle and admire our private paradise. "You've brought me to heaven."

Luke tugs off his shoes and settles on the blanket, patting the space next to him invitingly. "This is one of my favorite places to visit during the summer."

I quickly slide off my sandals and take a seat next to him, enjoying the comforting feel of cool earth beneath my feet.

Our secluded little area feels nice and balmy, with a mild breeze and ample sunshine. Tugging off my hoodie, I stretch out on the blanket to absorb more of the golden warmth.

Luke proceeds to point out the various wildflowers, from bright yellow monkey flowers to magenta wild roses to brilliant red-orange coast lilies.

Unzipping the backpack, he pulls out a couple of turkey and avocado sandwiches, a container of quinoa salad and two bottles of water.

I unwrap a sandwich and take a bite, admiring the emerald green hummingbirds hovering around the pale purple milkweed flowers.

"Does owning Poppy Bay Cottages take up a lot of your time?" I ask between bites of the sandwich. "It seems like it would be a lot of work, with upkeep and managing guests and such."

Luke scoops some quinoa salad onto a small plate. "I work with a property management company that handles the cottages and a couple of other vacation rentals in Poppy Bay, so it's not too all-consuming. But things can get busy and need my direct involvement at times." He takes a bite of salad and chews thoughtfully before continuing. "I think the commercial properties in San Francisco take up more of my time, and I do take frequent trips down there for work."

I give him an appraising look. "You have commercial properties in San Francisco? Sounds lucrative."

He nods. "It can be lucrative. When our parents transitioned, I didn't want Christine or Holly to ever worry about basic needs. I skipped college and went straight into real estate. I learned that I'm actually really good at it."

There's no arrogance coming from Luke about his last statement; it sounds as though he's just genuinely stating the truth.

I smile at him and say, "It sounds like you found something that was a good match for you."

He gives a short laugh. "When you're the sole provider of two other lives, you learn to get your shit together pretty quickly. If it hadn't been for my parents passing, I likely would have been a wayward son, without any real direction in life."

I set my sandwich down and contemplate him for a moment. "I really admire you, Luke. Holly and Christine are lucky to have you for their brother, and for how well you've taken care of them."

He shrugs. "It's what needed to be done, and I feel really fortunate to have them in my life."

I motion my hands down Luke's long body, thinking about his many admirers at the market earlier today. "Your whole story gives you a kind of handsome widower sex appeal, one that I'm sure many people find very attractive."

Luke slants me a sidelong glance, but he says nothing.

A flash of guilt cracks through me at my crass words, and I immediately back-pedal. "Crap Luke, I'm sorry. It is so inappropriate for me to make light of such a tragedy, and I'm really just very sorry. I shouldn't have said that."

A small smile quirks at the corner of his mouth. "You think I have sex appeal?"

41

My remorseful expression melts into an inquisitive one while I study his face. The mirth twinkling in his eyes tells me very clearly that he's trying to hold in laughter.

My lips press into a thin line while I try and contain my own laughter; I'm so glad he's taking my faux pas in stride.

He lifts a brow in question—still seemingly waiting for my "sex appeal" response—and I say nothing, the heat warming my face having nothing to do with the brilliant sunshine. Finally, I nod.

He watches the sea with a smile touching his profile and takes a drink of his water.

"I like that you see the lighter side of darkness," he says, turning to meet my gaze. "It's a good quality to have."

Relief courses through me, and I collapse onto the blanket, staring up at the cerulean blue sky. "Thank you."

Luke lies down next to me, and we both watch the cotton white clouds drift across the sky. Butterflies are flitting around us, bees are humming gently near the flowers, and the stream is a flowing background melody. Everything here feels sublime—being with Luke, being with the wildflowers and of course, being by the sea.

After comfortable silence stretches easily between us, I tell Luke that I met Alejandro today at Sunny Sea Bistro, and he begins to regale me with amusing tales of his childhood shenanigans with Alejandro.

I share stories about my travels—leaving out my search for other merfolk—and about the places I have yet to visit but plan to someday.

The sun begins to dip low in the sky, and a chill takes the air. I turn on my side to watch Luke's profile, admiring the strong lines of his jaw, until he also turns on his side to face me.

We observe each other for a few moments, and my heart swells for the absolute perfection of this day.

"Did you know there are little flecks of gold in your eyes?" he asks softly. "I noticed them yesterday at the pool; you can only see them in the sunshine."

"Yes, it's unusual, huh? All of that gold amid the dark brown."

He trails a finger down the side of my face, and my breath catches at his light touch.

"It's captivating, and almost..."

"Almost?" My voice is scarcely a whisper—desire is sweeping over me in a gigantic wave, and having Luke this close is like getting caught in a wild undertow of need.

"Almost...otherworldly." Luke's blue eyes darken to a midnight sky, and travel down to my lips.

Remembering my resolve to not enmesh romantically with him, I sit up abruptly and break the connection between us.

I put my hoodie back on and rub my arms briskly. "It's starting to feel a little cold. Can we head back?"

Luke immediately sits up. "Sure yes, of course."

He begins to pack up our picnic items, and a little piece of my heart cracks at his instantaneous appeasing of my request—it feels like acquiescence with perhaps a touch of defeat.

Luke gets everything into the backpack while I fold the blanket. We trek back down the hill, through the redwoods and to the parking area that now only has a couple of

43

vehicles. We get into the truck and begin the drive back to Poppy Bay.

"Thank you for inviting me today," I say. "I had a great time."

Luke's attention doesn't leave the winding curves of the coastal road, but he says, "I'm glad, Lullaby. It was fun for me too."

There's amiable silence for the rest of the drive; I watch the twilight ocean while Luke navigates the harrowing curves with the skilled ease of someone who has done it a million times before.

When we arrive at Luke's house, he walks me back to my cottage. At the driveway he hesitates, as though he wants to say something.

Peering up at him, I ask, "What is it?"

He gives me a half-smile. "I was just wondering if you'd like to come over for dinner tomorrow? We can eat on the terrace and watch the sunset from there."

My heart leaps at the invitation, while my head warns to keep my distance.

"Dinner sounds fantastic," I say, bypassing my head and gleefully giving my heart full license. "I'd love to join you."

Luke smiles; it's all charm and goodness and light. "Great, I'll see you then."

With a wave, I enter the cottage and stride straight for a shower because yes, I want to feel Luke's hot fantasy kisses all over my body again.

When I'm finished I collapse into bed and, feeling marginally sated, wonder how long I can really keep up this charade of restraint.

Chapter 7

I spend most of the next day visiting shops on Main Street and walking along the beach.

When it's time to meet Luke for dinner, I return to the cottage and change into gray jeans and a sapphire blue fitted sweater. Slipping on a pair of black ballet flats, I grab the crudité platter I picked up from the market and walk the trail to Luke's house.

Luke answers the door with a warm smile and kitchen towel slung over his shoulder. He's barefoot in jeans and a long-sleeved black Henley that looks soft and comfy.

I take a seat at the kitchen island and munch on cucumber and radish slices while Luke finalizes our meal. He has made us creamy polenta, roasted broccoli, and an entrée salad with sauteed mushrooms, butternut squash and toasted walnuts.

"Do you like to cook?" Luke asks, glancing up from the salad he's tossing with balsamic vinaigrette.

"No," I reply with a quick laugh. "I prefer to assemble my meals rather than actually cook them—salads, wraps, sandwiches and such. Do you enjoy cooking?"

"When I have time, I do. It's relaxing for me."

I have noticed how at ease Luke appears in the kitchen, like one of those rare souls who can cook *and* converse at the same time. That is not the case with me at all; I generally find cooking to be a stressful endeavor, with the stress greatly amplified if there's also an audience to entertain.

"Everything looks amazing," I comment, admiring the abundance of goodies he's made for us. "My mouth is watering just looking at it."

Luke wipes his hands on the kitchen towel. "It's all ready, so we can take it upstairs now."

We both fill individual salad bowls and side plates, and carry them upstairs to the rooftop terrace.

"It is fantastic up here," I say when we step onto the roof. The overall design is understated like the rest of Luke's house, which allows the stunning view of the bay to take center stage. There are a few potted plants dotting the terrace, a small round dining table, slate gray sofa and two matching chairs. Three elegant warming lamps are creating a nice buffer to the nippy breeze rippling across the space.

We set everything on the dining table, and Luke makes one more trip downstairs to bring up our beverages. There are cloth napkins and cutlery already arranged neatly on the table.

We sit down to eat, and I heartily savor every delectable morsel Luke has made. The polenta is rich and buttery, the broccoli is crisp and flavorful, and the salad is like a scrumptious buffet of nourishment for my body.

I take a break from feasting to sip some of my water, and Luke sets down his fork to swipe his napkin across his mouth.

"With all of the traveling you've done," he says, "I've been wondering if you're joyfully exploring the world, or if on a deeper level you're really searching for something?"

I set down my water glass with a grin. "You weren't kidding — you really aren't big on small talk."

"Too personal too fast?"

I shake my head. "No. You're the first person to ask me that, actually. It's a very perceptive question."

Luke leans back and takes a drink from his water glass, patiently waiting for me to respond. I look at the bay, watching the waves for a few pensive moments.

"Probably more of the latter," I finally say, my voice somewhat subdued.

"What are you searching for?" His voice is soft and unobtrusive.

I continue gazing out at the sea, with infinite longing now tugging at my heart. Turning to meet his eyes, I say, "Home."

Luke exhales a breath and nods, but he doesn't say anything.

I continue, "I enjoy traveling immensely; I really love the adventure and discovery of it. But, I do feel like it would be nice to have somewhere I…" My voice trails off, and I'm stunned to discover I'm actually blinking away tears.

"Somewhere you feel like you belong?" Luke offers gently.

My head dips and I twist the napkin on my lap. "Yes." I glance up and see Luke watching me with kind knowing in his eyes.

"In a way, I understand where you're coming from. Once Christine was married and Holly left for college, I felt

47

a little bit of empty nest syndrome. They had been my entire focus for most of my adult life, and aside from real estate, I wasn't really sure who I was or where I belonged." He smiles. "So I started to travel. I spent a year visiting London, Rome, Paris, Tokyo, New York and other places. I think I was trying to find a sense of belonging as well, but everything kept bringing me back here to Poppy Bay. It's not a big city by any stretch of the imagination, but it has everything: the ocean, redwoods, abundant plant and animal life, clean air and easy access to bigger city amenities."

"Poppy Bay is idyllic," I concur. "I actually prefer smaller coastal towns to big cities. But that was quite a bit of traveling for you; do you still enjoy it?"

Luke folds his hands behind his head and leans back in his chair. "I love traveling. And I also enjoy being here at home."

"I'd like to find that balance for myself at some point." My lips curl up into a crafty smile. "Maybe Poppy Bay can be my home — do you offer long-term rentals?"

Luke's mouth quirks at the corner, and his eyes gleam with either pleasure or desire, I'm not entirely certain. "For you, Lullaby? Absolutely."

"That's good to know." My tone is light, though my heart is beginning to thrum out a few staccato beats. Setting my napkin on the table, I give my full belly an affectionate rub. "I'm finished eating. Thank you so much for making everything, it was delicious."

Luke stands and grabs a couple of plates. "It's perfect timing; the sunset is about to begin."

I help Luke carry the plates down to the kitchen. We rinse the plates, load them into the dishwasher and pack up the leftovers for the fridge. Luke makes us a couple of cups of fragrant fennel tea; we bring them back up to the terrace and sit on the sofa to watch the sunset.

We are sitting close to one another on the sofa, so close that our thighs are touching. The contact feels both intimate and casually comfortable. We're both quiet as streaks of orange, violet and magenta race across the sky, chasing the sun ever lower into the horizon.

I keep shifting to steal glimpses of Luke's divine profile, and each time my head tilts towards him I see that he's already watching me.

"What?" I ask, pressing my lips together to prevent a spate of giggles. It seems that Luke not only draws deep feelings out of me, but exquisite bouts of silliness as well.

His brows lift, and his eyes are all twinkly with mischief and mirth. "I could ask you the same question."

With a chuckle, I set my tea on the side table and move to sit on his lap. "I think I need a boost, it will give me a better view." It's really not the truth, seeing as the glorious sunset is visible from even the floor, but it does give me an excuse to get closer to him.

"Come on over," he says, drawing me onto his jeans with ease.

I settle onto his lap, and he wraps his arms around my waist. My head is astonishingly silent; there are no objections, no warnings, nothing but blissful quiet. Which is great because my heart is positively singing with pleasure at being so cozy with Luke. Being in his arms feels perfect, and right.

"Better?" he asks near my ear, his breath caressing a sensual line down my neck.

"It's perfect," I murmur, snuggling deeper into his embrace. He smells like a sunlit forest—fresh, warm and woodsy.

We continue watching the sunset, all while the desire roiling about inside of me starts to reach a boiling point. Being in Luke's arms is great, but I want more.

"Luke?" I ask, still watching the darkening sky.

"Yes?"

"I want to kiss you."

I can feel his smile even from behind me. "If you're asking for my consent, Lullaby, then you've got it."

I turn on his lap and peer into his eyes, as though the solution to my dilemma lies within them.

He plays with a few strands of my hair. "What is it?"

I inhale a breath and decide to be forthcoming with him. "You are incredible, like *dream man* amazing. And you don't really strike me as a casual affair kind of person." I trace the line of his jaw, enjoying the feel of dark stubble beneath my fingers. "I'm only here for one month though, and I don't know where I'm going next but I do know that I will leave. And this is probably going to sound presumptuous and maybe even a little hubristic, but I want to let you know that I'm not available for anything serious or long term right now."

Luke tucks a strand of hair behind my ear and studies me for a few moments with compassion in his eyes. A soft smile curves on one side of his lips.

"I appreciate you being clear about that," he says. "Maybe though, it's not important if this is long term. Maybe it's more important that we're happy now."

I grin at his echo of my words about Holly's relationship. "Wise words."

His fingers trail down my cheek. "They're the wisdom of a beautiful person I recently met, someone I find thoroughly intriguing." Curling his fingers into my hair, he draws me close, his lips brushing mine in a feather-light kiss. "I want you to know that you don't have to protect me, Lullaby. I'm not fragile."

I can agree with him on that last point—based on the stiff ridge pressing into my backside, I would say that Luke is anything but fragile.

"I'm glad we clarified that," I murmur. Twisting on his lap so that I'm straddling him, I press my body into his and kiss him, long and deep and hard. And *oh God*, it is just the most toe-curling, breath-stealing, electric kiss I have ever experienced in my life. Luke's lips are skilled and supple, and when he runs his tongue across mine he tastes like sweet fennel.

I dig my fingers into his hair and deepen the kiss, rocking my hips onto his arousal and evoking a satisfying groan of pleasure from him. I'm just about to suggest that we head downstairs to his bedroom when something shocking reaches my awareness—something that vibrates through every single bone in my body.

Chapter 8

It's a mermaid call.

I don't hear it audibly, though if I were underwater I would hear it as extraordinarily deep notes. Instead, up here on land I feel it within my body and my soul.

Lifting my head from the kiss, I listen intently with my eyes closed to see if the call occurs again.

"What is it?" Luke asks, stroking his hands down the length of my hair.

There it is again, a siren song. Or a masculine merperson call, judging by the deep tone of the notes. Notes that are flowing from the depths of the sea to reach me, right here and right now.

"Shoot," I mutter, disentangling myself from Luke and standing abruptly. "I have to go."

Luke's eyes crease with great perplexity. "Is everything okay?"

I lean down to place a swift peck onto his lips, hope unfurling in my chest like a brilliant blossoming flower. "Everything is terrific. I just remembered I have to take care of something."

Luke moves to stand as well, but I stop him. "It's okay, I'll show myself out."

I start to make a swift exit then pause and turn around, catching his baffled expression. I can only imagine how he feels—one moment we're immersed in a passionate embrace and the next, poof! I'm dashing off with a vague excuse.

"Can I see you tomorrow?" I ask. I really want him to know that this is not me skipping out on him.

"I'm going to San Francisco for work tomorrow; I'll be staying there overnight."

Some of my joy deflates. "Okay, text me when you return?"

Luke nods, then peers at me with inquisitive eyes. "Are you sure everything is okay?"

With a cheerful wave, I stride to the stairs leading down into his house. "Everything is great! I'll see you when you get back."

I grab my purse from the living room and leave Luke's house. I take the path that leads back to my cottage, just in case Luke is watching me from the terrace. As soon as I emerge from the trees and reach Wild Rose Cottage, I quickly change course and cut across the sand dunes towards the beach.

I pass Luke's house, staying close to the water to ensure my nighttime concealment, and jog to the northern part of the bay where the large rocks are all clustered.

Choosing a tall boulder that is partially in the bay, I scurry up it and wake several sleeping seagulls in the process. They squawk at being disturbed before flying off the rock.

"Sorry friends," I say, peering out into the inky water.

The gulls circle the boulder a few times then land on it again. They watch me warily while I strip all of my clothes off, closing their eyes once I'm naked.

Without a second glance back, I dive into the water and immediately shift into my mermaid form.

I zoom out past the bay and into the depths of the sea, trying to pinpoint where I heard the call coming from. I even open my mermaid intuition, but true to my previous experiences attempting to use it underwater, it feels muted and ineffective.

I send out my call, with the crystalline notes high and light and filled with oceans of hope. And, I wait.

There's a haunting and ethereal response in return, and with a pounding heart I swim towards the notes.

I arrive at the source of the responding call—it's a blue whale mama and her calf. The pair are indescribably beautiful, like two celestial beings floating in a halcyon sea. The mama is singing to her calf; I must have mistook her dulcet lullaby for another mermaid call.

How could I have done that?

Blue whale sounds are very deep, and it should have been obvious to me that it was a whale call. Since I've never actually heard another merperson's call I guess it is possible for me to mistake whale calls for one.

But still. I've always felt that I would inherently know when it was coming from a merperson, like it would vibrate into my bones and soul as it did tonight.

I send a few notes of greeting to the mama whale, who pulses several serene notes to me in return. The pair are so very lovely, and their combined energy is incredibly gentle, even though I feel like a tiny minnow next to them.

With a wave of my shimmering tail, I turn and begin to swim back towards the bay, all the while tempering my disappointment so as not to perturb the highly perceptive mama and her calf with the heaviness of my mood.

I keep my energy in check until I reach the bay, then I shift into human form and exit the water. I climb the rock where I left my clothes and get dressed with leaden movements.

I walk along the beach for a bit, with the despondency growing so heavy within me that I can't even hold myself upright. Right near the shore, I collapse onto the sand.

With my hands cradling my head, I begin to cry. And not little weepy tears either, I mean big messy choking sobs. Gut-wrenching and heart-wrenching sobs.

I really just cannot explain the ache of loss that has been haunting me for so many years now — for my merparents, and for other merpeople like me.

For not the first time in my life, I feel completely and utterly alone.

How can I possibly be the only merperson left on the entire planet? I cannot fathom it; it's a loneliness so great it feels immeasurable.

My deep sobs are masked by the soothing sound of the waves, but there is nothing at all soothing about the violent shudders convulsing throughout my entire body.

"Lullaby?" Luke's voice gently interrupts my seaside meltdown.

With a start, I jerk up to see him standing a few feet away from me, and even in the darkness I can feel the concern radiating from him in deep waves.

He takes a few steps towards me, and I quickly wipe the tears from my cheeks.

"Hi Luke," I say, attempting and royally failing to speak in a normal voice that is not choked with anguish. "Are you enjoying your evening walk?"

Kneeling down, he strokes my hair, making no comment about how wet it is. "I am, but are you okay?" His eyes seem to be searching mine for the answer.

I shake my head. No, I'm not okay, but how do I explain it to Luke?

Deciding simplicity is the best option, I say, "I miss my family." I shift my attention out to sea so he doesn't catch too much of the pain that must be apparent in my eyes.

Luke says nothing. Instead, he sits on the wet sand behind me, with his knees bent on the sides of my waist. Wrapping his arms around me, he draws me close to his chest and kisses the back of my head.

The warmth and comfort of his embrace has me melting into him with a shuddering breath.

"It's okay," he murmurs. "It's okay to miss them."

Emotion floods me at his absolute tenderness, and a new slew of tears spills out of my eyes.

Nestling deep into Luke's chest, I allow myself to cry, and cry some more. I sob openly while he holds me and hums quiet words of comfort to me.

Finally, when I feel the catharsis of shedding so many tears, we stand and walk to Wild Rose Cottage. This time

Luke comes in with me, turning on the fire in the hearth to chase away the chill of the living room.

"I'm going to take a shower," I tell him, with deep waves of fatigue sweeping through every limb of my body. I'm almost too exhausted to even shower, but I really want to wash the ocean salt off of me.

Luke immediately starts for the front door. "I'll just go."

I reach out for his arm and gently stop him from opening the door. "Will you join me in the water?"

Luke's pupils dilate, and his eyes search mine while several layers of sentiment flit across his face: affection, compassion, need.

"Okay," he says simply.

I take his hand and lead him down the hallway. We undress in my bedroom, then Luke starts the shower and guides me under the soothing hot stream. He must sense how absolutely depleted I feel, because instead of seducing me in the shower, he washes my hair and body with a chaste tenderness that feels a lot like love.

And still, each time I shift in the stall I bump into his erection, which is occupying a rather large amount of space between us. So the desire pulsing in our midst is not *entirely* lost on my slumberous mind.

Luke finishes his gentle ministrations and turns off the water, bundling me up in a thick white robe that swishes around my ankles. He wraps a towel around his lean waist, and I lift onto my toes to tuck an errant wave of his chestnut hair off his forehead.

"Thank you," I whisper to him, feeling great affection tangled with bone-deep exhaustion. If this were any other night, I'm positive the shower would have gone much differently. But I'm glad I was vulnerable with Luke—it feels like it's made our connection sweeter and deeper than it would have been otherwise.

Luke draws me into the bedroom and pulls back the covers on the bed. I crawl in and invite him to join me.

He lies behind me and contours his whole body around mine, telling me quietly, "I don't have to go to San Francisco tomorrow. I can schedule it for another day and be here with you instead."

My heart melts for his kind offer, and I nuzzle deeper into his embrace. "I'll be okay; you can go tomorrow. Just be here with me tonight, please."

Luke's mouth brushes the back of my neck in a delicate kiss, and my eyes flutter closed. His hand begins to caress my hair with placid strokes, and I sink into a deep and welcome sleep.

Chapter 9

The next morning Luke leaves the cottage at dawn, offering again to stay in Poppy Bay.

"I'm feeling much better," I tell him while standing on the front porch, and it's the truth. All of that crying and cuddling and sleeping in his solid embrace worked wonders on my deflated state of mind. "Thank you for everything last night; I appreciate it more than words can say."

"It's my pleasure," he says, entwining his fingers in mine and brushing a light kiss across my knuckles.

I peer over at Holly's cottage, half expecting window curtains to quickly fall back into place. But Trillium Cottage is dark and still at this early hour.

Noticing the direction of my gaze, Luke's eyes crinkle at the corners. "She usually sleeps in late when she's here."

I give a little laugh. "I guess I wouldn't mind if Holly saw us together anyway. Would you?"

"Not at all. I'm sure it would make her day." With one more brush of his lips on my hand he says, "I'll text you when I get back."

I wave as he leaves the porch and takes the trail into the pine trees, while no small part of my heart whispers that it already misses him.

I enter the cottage and make a cup of lemon balm tea, mentally planning my activities for the day. Once the sun has fully risen and Poppy Bay is awash in its golden rays, I get dressed, pack some snacks and set off for the beach.

Unfolding a large towel on the sand, I slip off my shoes and recline back on the towel.

The early morning sunshine feels marvelous on my cool skin. With a deep inhale of the salubrious sea air, I close my eyes and soak up the solar blessings. I may even doze off for a spell, because when I open my eyes again, the number of families on the beach—with screeching children and equally ecstatic dogs—has greatly increased.

Sitting up, I wrap my arms around my knees and peer out at the water. The rhythmic movement of the waves is almost hypnotic, and I allow myself to just ebb and flow with them…easy in, easy out.

There's a tickle near my pinky toe, and I look down to see a tiny hermit crab marching over my foot. With my breath held and sitting still as stone, I let the hermit crab journey across my foot and into a nearby tide pool.

Goodness, I really do love this place. There's beauty to be found in every corner, and even without other fellow merfolk there's a certain sort of magic to Poppy Bay that is very appealing to me.

I can almost see myself setting up a home base here— spending my days creating new travel content with a glorious view of the bay, taking breaks to go into town or the beach, swimming as a mermaid in the sea at night, being with Luke, exploring new places with him.

I really wasn't anticipating Luke when I decided to take this sabbatical from work, though to say that I'm glad I met him would be putting it mildly.

Last night felt like a tipping point for us, like things shifted from just casual to profoundly significant. For all of my searching around the globe for others like me, I seem to have found a kindred soul in Luke the human. And there's a great part of me that wants to explore more of that connection with him.

I pull some celery sticks and a small container of cashew butter out of my beach bag. Dipping a celery stick in the nut butter, I take a bite and watch the hermit crab interact with a few other ones in the tide pool.

What if I were to tell Luke that I'm a mermaid?

I've never told anyone that before, except for my dad. The first time I shifted was when I was going through puberty, so with my first period came my first tail, while I was taking a bath at home.

I didn't actually know I was a mermaid prior to that, though I always felt that I was different, I just wasn't sure exactly how.

When I first shifted into my mermaid form, it wasn't a terrifying shock or anything like that, it was really more of a relief. I felt like, "Okay, this is why I feel so different from everyone else. Because I am!"

Shortly after that, I shifted for my dad in our pool at home—wearing a bikini top for coverage—and even he seemed a little relieved.

He took the transformation in relative stride, saying that it explained a lot of my "unique qualities", and it's been our secret ever since.

I've never even really wanted to tell anyone else; having relationships that don't get much closer than arm's length don't really inspire that level of disclosure.

Dad is aware that the bulk of Lullaby's Travels has been dedicated to finding other merpeople, whether on land or in the sea. And since Dad is a mythology professor in Boston, he's been super helpful with the local mermaid lore for most of the places I've visited.

But all of that secrecy and searching... Now it's just starting to feel like a great anchor around my neck, like how many more places can I search, how many more calls can I send out, before I finally give up?

What if I were to continue Lullaby's Travels purely for the joy of it? For the joy of visiting new places and immersing into new cultures, without any other agenda.

The business overall is very profitable for me, with most of my income being passive in the form of book royalties and travel lifestyle business courses, so financially I'm amply comfortable.

If Luke and I were in a dedicated relationship, it wouldn't be fair to either of us if I went dashing off at the slightest hint of other merpeople, like I did last night. And something deep within me is saying that my search is not yet over.

I can still feel a pulse of my merparents within my cells, and even though my adoption was closed and I know nothing about my biological parents, Dad once told me that perhaps one of my parents is human while the other is a merperson. That doesn't really ring true to me, though.

I know on a soul-deep level that both of my biological parents are merpeople, mainly because even though I live a very human life, I have never really felt like a human being. And if there's still a chance that I can find them someday, then is that something I *want* to give up on?

I won't deny the feelings I have for Luke though, or how they are deepening every day. But if I were to truly explore a committed relationship with him, then I would have to tell him I'm a mermaid, and that thought is terrifying.

The idea of mermaids may be sexy and mystical, but being with one in real life brings a whole new level of complication. And complicated is not something I do well, or at all. Not to mention the danger it places me in.

If too many people found out about me, I could be captured and studied by humans who view me as nothing more than a research specimen, or worse.

I continue munching on the celery sticks and cashew butter, watching the waves curl and dissipate into the surf.

Most of my adult life has been lived just like a wave — flowing into a new place and flowing out. Flowing into a new romantic affair and flowing out. Never staying in one place or with one person long enough for things to get messy.

But maybe, it's time for that to change?

I don't have all the answers now, but I'm willing to keep my heart open to harmonious possibilities in the meantime.

Curling my index finger in a little wave to the hermit crabs, I pack up my snacks and towel, and walk back to the cottage.

Chapter 10

It's after midnight when I leave the cottage for a swim.

I walk to where the large boulders are clustered on the north end of the bay; tucking my clothes and a towel between two smaller rocks, I enter the dark water and shift into my mermaid form.

I swim over the graceful leopard sharks feeding on the sandy floor, through the dense kelp forest and into the open sea.

Sending out my mermaid call, I listen for a response.

Deep, serene notes answer my call, and with a smile I swim to the summer feeding area of the mama blue whale and her calf.

I offer to babysit the darling calf while mama whale rests, and she gratefully accepts the offer. Baby and I spend most of our time together playing with large bubble rings that I blow in the water. We also sing to each other, softly so as not to disturb his resting mama.

It's a terrific time overall, and before I leave mama and baby, I ask mama whale via pulsed notes if she has encountered any other merfolk in her travels.

Mama's gentle response is for me to keep my heart open, and there's a wisdom illuminating her gaze that I cannot even begin to comprehend.

She tells me that love is the most important thing in life—no matter the form it takes.

I have received similar messages from other whales throughout the world's oceans, and though it is not precisely the response my head wants to hear, ultimately it's the response that is the most comforting to my heart.

Thanking mama whale for her guidance, I wish her and baby well on their continued migration. I swim back to the bay, feeling a small flutter of hope in my heart.

Even if there aren't any other merfolk left on this planet, at least I have other sea life that I can joyfully connect with, and of course, humans like Luke. The thought has me smiling all the way back to Wild Rose Cottage.

* * *

I get a text message from Luke early the next afternoon letting me know he's back from San Francisco.

As soon as I read it, I leave the cottage barefoot and jog the trail to his house, my heart thrumming eagerly in anticipation of seeing him again.

My pace slows a bit when his driveway comes into view, and I begin to feel the slightest bit ridiculous in my untethered enthusiasm.

Luke's truck is in the driveway; he's just exiting it, with a backpack slung over one shoulder.

As soon as he sees me at the trailhead his eyes light up like a midnight sun, while my insides melt into a puddle of sappy goo.

I'm also suddenly feeling shy; the vulnerability I shared with him two nights ago has me feeling more exposed than standing naked with him in the shower.

"Did you just get back?" I ask in a casual tone, one that belies the nerves and giddiness vibrating throughout my body.

"Yes, I texted you right when I pulled up." He peers down at my bare feet and grins. "Did you run over here as soon as you got my text?"

With a throaty giggle, I reply, "Yes."

"So we are equally enthusiastic then." Setting his backpack on the hood of his truck, he opens his arms and beckons me to him. "Come here."

With a wide smile, I cross the distance and wrap my arms around his neck in a tight embrace. Lifting me off of my feet, he kisses me, deeply and slowly.

"Is it weird to say that I missed you?" I ask after we part, feeling breathless and a little dizzy with joy.

He sets me down, touching his forehead to mine. "No, I felt the same." Straightening, he says, "I couldn't stop thinking about you while I was gone; it was actually kind of distracting from my work."

I know the feeling.

Last night while in bed I kept replaying the shower scene with Luke. Except in this version, I did much more than just bump into his erection. The vivid mental imagery combined with Luke's scent all over my pillows brought me to climax in about two seconds flat.

The calescent glint in Luke's eyes tells me I'm likely not the only one who reimagined that scene.

"I would apologize for being such a distraction to you, but that would be disingenuous of me." I am actually utterly pleased to have been on his mind so much. "Were you able to get *some* work done at least?"

Luke chuckles. "I appreciate your honesty, and yes, I was able to get work done."

"Hey guys!" Holly, Kendra and Min-Jun are approaching from the end of the driveway; they are each carrying a beach bag and towel. Holly continues, "Luke, can we swim in the pool? The water's too cold at the swimming beach today."

Luke points to the front door of his house. "Of course."

Holly starts walking towards the entrance then pauses. "Did you invite Lullaby to my back-to-school barbecue?"

"I hadn't gotten to that yet," Luke replies, "but yes, I was going to invite her."

Holly peers at me with a hopeful smile. "It's tomorrow here at the house; can you make it? It was kind of a last minute plan."

I nod. "Yes, I'd love to attend."

"Great!" Holly waves and pulls a set of keys out of her beach bag. She unlocks the front door, and Kendra and Min-Jun follow her into the house.

"Would you like to come swimming with us?" Luke asks me. "Holly and crew are likely to be here for a while."

"That sounds great; I just have to go grab a swimsuit."

Luke's brow furrows. "Is that necessary? We've already seen each other naked."

My forehead creases in mild confusion, and I peer at the backyard fence where laughter and splashes can now be heard from the other side.

Where does he want to swim naked together? Surely not with Holly and her partners.

When I look back at Luke I catch the teasing laughter in his eyes.

"Cheeky," I mutter, playfully pushing his shoulder. "I'll be right back."

I trot over to my cottage, and just to get under Luke's skin, I grab my teeniest tiniest black bikini that is about as close to naked as I'm going to get in polite company. With a gleeful smile, I walk back along the trail to spend a full and fun day at Luke's house.

Chapter 11

The next day, I meet Luke at his house in the early afternoon to help set up for the barbecue.

None of the guests have arrived yet, and we spend most of the time chopping fresh vegetables for the grill and preparing a massive potato salad.

Holly, Kendra and Min-Jun arrive just as we're beginning to set out plates, cutlery and beverages on the picnic table in the backyard. Together we complete setting the table, then Luke and I head back into the kitchen to finalize the meal components. Holly and her partners remain under the pergola, with Holly and Min-Jun slathering layers of sunblock on Kendra's porcelain skin.

I'm loading a few dishes into the dishwasher when Luke suddenly steps up behind me and wraps his arms around my waist. I shift in his arms to face him, and he leans down to kiss me with slow, deliberate tenderness.

"I've been wanting to do that all day," he murmurs when we part. "We've just been so busy getting everything set up."

I nuzzle into his neck, inhaling his scent that is like golden sunshine woven into a spring forest, and take a little lick of his skin, just to see if he tastes like it too.

His breath hitches with the touch of my tongue, and I suckle my way up his neck and jaw until I reach his mouth for a kiss. He lifts me onto the island with ease, deepening our kiss and positioning himself between my thighs. My arms reach up to encircle his neck, and one of his hands grips into my hair with just enough pressure to melt me right into his body.

Luke's other hand trails under my shirt, up my waist and to my bra. The pad of his thumb grazes my nipple through the thin fabric, evoking a whimper of need from deep within me.

The sound of the front door opening reaches us, and we pull apart just in time to see Christine, her husband Omari and their two young children entering the kitchen.

Luke and I are both breathless at this point, and my hair must be a tousled mess. With a quick adjustment of my t-shirt, I hop down from the island and grab a hand towel, pretending to wipe an invisible smudge on the counter.

Luke grins at my instant innocent action, and Christine lifts a brow, her eagle eye missing absolutely nothing.

She introduces me to Omari—who is a handsome man with wire-framed glasses, dark brown skin and a friendly smile—and their two adorable children.

Christine and her family vacate the kitchen through the sliding glass door, with the children running straight for the pool. I toss the towel onto the counter and cover my face with my hands.

"That's not really how I wanted to meet your sister's family," I mutter between my fingers.

Luke laughs and pulls me into a hug. "It's okay; I'm an adult with my own personal life."

I draw back and peer up at him. He doesn't appear to be at all bothered by the situation; he actually seems fairly amused by it instead.

"You're right," I concede. "I'm going to grab a bathing suit at the cottage. I'll be back in a bit."

Luke's eyes darken with desire. "Please tell me you're wearing the black bikini again. *Please.*"

"No," I say with a chuckle. "It's not really appropriate for a family gathering. I know Holly and the college kids complimented it, but I'm not sure how Christine would feel about me parading around in that tiny thing in front of her husband and two young children."

"I'm sure Omari would appreciate it just fine," he retorts.

I give an admonishing squeeze to his bicep. "He is your sister's *husband.*"

He plants a swift peck on my lips. "I'm kidding."

There's a knock at the front door, then it opens and Sunny and Alejandro emerge from the foyer.

"Hello!" Sunny greets us with a wide smile. Today his silver-white hair is fastened with two pretty seashell clips.

I give him and Alejandro a hug, then make my exit while Luke takes them out to the backyard to join the others.

At the cottage, I strip out of my tee and jean shorts, slide into my burgundy one-piece swimsuit and put the clothes back on before walking the trail back to Luke's house.

71

There seems to be an intense conversation taking place near his backyard gate, based on what I can hear from the trail. The heated, low tones slow my pace along the path, and I peek around the cluster of trees to see who it is.

It's Christine and Luke.

Christine looks serious per usual, but Luke appears to be distraught, per not usual.

I take a few soundless steps closer to them — still mostly hidden by the trees — and try to hear what they're saying.

I know that eavesdropping isn't really a great practice to engage in, but something about Luke's expression has me feeling worried. Not to mention the strong feeling I'm getting that their conversation is about me.

"If she is what you think she is," Christine is telling Luke, "then you know what you have to do."

Luke rakes a hand through his hair. "I'm not sure yet… I need more time."

Holy hell, are they talking about me being a mermaid? A band of apprehension tightens around my body, and I lean forward to hear more of their conversation.

Christine says, "You don't have much more time; the meteor shower is in four days."

Scrubbing a hand down his face, Luke replies in a resigned voice, "I know."

Christine lays a hand on his forearm. "And you know what comes after that. It's the right thing to do, Luke."

Deciding that I've heard enough, I stride out of the concealment of the trees to where they're standing. My hands are shaking with adrenaline, so I clasp them in front of me to calm the tremors.

Christine slants me an inscrutable look that is either pity, compassion, or a blend of the two. With a penetrating look at Luke, she walks to the fence gate, opens it and enters the backyard.

The gate clicks quietly behind her. I look up at Luke, who seems to be avoiding my gaze.

Without preamble, I ask, "Was that about me?"

Luke regards me for a few moments then nods. "Yes."

I inhale a fragmented breath. "Are you going to hurt me?" I'm attempting to keep my voice even, but it still sounds tremulous to my ears.

Luke's expression softens into tenderness. "No, Lullaby. I'm not going to hurt you."

His words feel mildly reassuring, but not entirely.

Luke continues, "I can assure you that you're safe here, and that you can trust me."

I nod once. "What happens during the meteor shower?"

Luke smiles, more of the tension leaving his face. "Stars fall from the sky and land in the sea."

I tilt my head in question, and he further explains, "When the meteor shower starts, jellyfish appear in the bay. They have bioluminescence that makes it look like the shooting stars are landing in the water. It's almost as though the jellyfish are lighting up in response to the meteors."

"Is that all that happens?"

"There's also a storm. Every year within three days of the meteor shower we get a big storm. It only lasts for a couple of hours, but it's wild."

I cross my arms over my chest. "I get the sense that you're not telling me the full story. But I do want to trust you."

Luke bridges the distance between us and takes both of my hands in a gentle grasp. "I want to tell you everything." He glances over his shoulder at the backyard, which sounds lively with an increased number of guests. "How about tomorrow morning? Can we talk then?"

"Okay." I don't really know what else to do at the moment but trust his word and hear him out tomorrow morning. I'd rather not abruptly leave Poppy Bay if I can help it; I really do love it here. But I'm going to tuck that option into my back pocket anyway, at least until I know precisely what is going on here.

"Thank you." He lays a light kiss on my temple and we walk through the gate into the backyard, where I endeavor to enjoy myself with the guests, many newly arrived who appear to be friends of Holly's.

My attention is only half on the jolly conversations though; the other half of my mind is trying to figure out what the heck Luke is not telling me, and what Christine has to do with any of it.

Maybe they weren't talking about me being a mermaid; maybe it was more about me being a "wandering spirit", as Sunny put it when he first met me. I really don't know for certain. But the meteor shower? What does that have to do with anything, including me being a mermaid?

By the time night falls, I'm feeling mentally exhausted. Pretending to engage in social niceties while internally swimming in a dark well of anxiety has been an exercise in total depletion.

I attempt to leave the backyard as inconspicuously as possible, but Luke must see me because he calls out to me as I'm walking the trail to my cottage.

I pause on the path and turn to him, meeting his gaze in the clear and cool night.

"I'll see you tomorrow morning, right?" he asks, his eyes soft and searching.

My chin dips in confirmation. "Yes."

Stepping closer to me, he says in a soothing tone, "It's going to be okay, Lullaby. I promise." He leans down, drawing me into a tentative embrace.

I welcome the embrace, lifting up to wrap my arms around his neck and inhale his comforting scent, hoping to all that is good and gracious in this world that he is telling the truth.

Chapter 12

Luke and I meet Holly, Kendra and Min-Jun at Trillium Cottage early the next morning.

"You'll stay in touch, right?" Holly asks me as we hug a final time. She and her partners are all packed up and just getting into Holly's car for the drive back to Cal State.

"I will, of course." My response may or may not be the truth, depending on what Luke reveals to me today.

Holly hasn't given any indication that she's privy to whatever Luke and Christine were discussing yesterday at the barbeque, and my sense is that they have not yet looped her into anything that pertains to me.

With a final wave, Holly pulls out of the driveway. Luke and I watch until her car disappears around a bend in the road, then we take the trail to his house.

We're both quiet on the path, though Luke does entwine his fingers in mine and cast affectionate smiles my way.

Everything about his energy feels calming and soothing today, like he's trying really hard to not startle me away.

It's working.

Despite the distress he exhibited during the initial conversation I overheard with Christine, he seems to be embodying a healthy measure of inner peace now. Which is flowing over to me and, however mildly, reassuring me that I may not be in any real danger.

We get into Luke's truck, and he takes the local road north, past the large boulders I normally use for cover when I'm shifting and swimming. We drive a few miles north of the bay, then Luke turns onto a narrow gravel road that ends in a small parking area.

He parks the truck and we both exit. Taking my hand in his, he leads me through a patch of redwood trees to a sequestered beach cove. There's a rocky jetty that extends far into the sea, and Luke guides me onto the jetty. With each step along the rocks, a sense of anticipation begins to build within me. I have no idea what the anticipation is for, but I'm feeling it nonetheless, like little pricks of electricity sparking within me.

Luke stops about halfway out and takes a seat on a flat boulder, extending his hand for me to join him. I take his proffered hand and sit next to him, studying his profile while he observes the ocean. His hair is fluttering in the cool breeze, and his expression is pensive. Ripples of water are lapping gently against the rocks on both sides of us.

"Shortly after my parents died," he says, still watching the sea, "I came out here to the jetty one night. I was feeling so much confusion, grief and anger. I couldn't understand how my parents could just leave us, me and Christine and Holly, who was only two years old at the time. I had no idea what my next steps were. I was only twenty, and even with the great age gap between me and Holly, I still knew nothing about caring for a toddler, or teenaged Christine."

I smooth a hand over Luke's hair and trail it down to his nape. He takes my hand and runs his lips across my palm.

"This was a couple of nights after the meteor shower," he continues. "A storm rose up from the sea very quickly, and it started to rain on me, hard. The winds were ferocious as well. I stood up on the rocks and I raged at the storm — in the same way I felt like it was raging at me. I screamed into the wind, I cursed my parents, cursed my life. I unleashed all of my grief onto the storm, which at that point felt like it was just a mirror of my own inner chaos."

I run my hand over his leg, silently encouraging him to continue.

"I shouted, I cried. The trees on the beach were bending and breaking in the wind, and the waves were so high and crashing all around me, but I didn't care. I think I wanted the storm to take me — to take the pain away from me. Instead, I got knocked over by a strong wind and hit my head on a rock. I think I was unconscious for a while. When I awoke, I could still see the storm raging on the shore and far out at sea, but all around me it was quiet and still. Almost as though I had been pushed into a funnel of calm."

Luke's eyes meet mine, and he smiles. "I looked down into the placid water, and that's when I saw it: Mermaid City." He chuckles. "Well, that's what I named it anyway. It was a glowing emerald city with merpeople swimming all around it, deep under the surface. Their tails were sparkling like starlight in the water, and I could see the various buildings that comprised the city."

My breath falters, and my heart begins to pound out a few staccato beats, but still I say nothing.

"At first I thought I was hallucinating, like something triggered by my fall. But I stayed there for hours and watched the city, and I knew I wasn't hallucinating. I knew that Mermaid City was real."

I'm attempting to maintain a neutral expression, but inside I'm quaking with a vortex of emotions. This is what Luke and Christine were talking about? An actual, real-life city of merpeople?

Luke continues, "The storm started to abate; I could see it subsiding on the shore and farther out in the ocean. The city started to disappear as well, like it was just dissolving in the water. When the storm was gone, so was the city." He leans back and exhales. "I don't really know what happened that night, but when I got back home I felt clarity, and peace. I knew that I wanted to become Christine and Holly's legal guardian; I wanted to keep us together as a family."

Linking my fingers with his, I say, "You were very brave."

He nods. "I felt brave. I also felt forgiveness in my heart for my parents, and I trusted that there was a greater plan at work. I've never really been a religious person, but I felt a divine presence working with, for and through me then. I felt confident about my next steps, and I knew that I wasn't alone in it."

I look out at the ocean, watching the waves with a great sense of wonder permeating my heart.

"The storm has come every year since," he says. "And every year I see Mermaid City, for only a couple of hours each time before it disappears. I think the meteor shower and storm are like a portal that opens the city; I'm not really sure how it all works."

Exhaling a deep breath, I turn to him and smile. "Thank you for telling me this."

Luke takes my hand in his, stroking along my palm. "Is this story relevant to you, Lullaby? Is Mermaid City relevant to you?"

I meet Luke's eye and swallow hard. This is my opportunity to tell him the truth, right here in this very moment. But goodness gracious I am *terrified*. Not for my safety, because it's obvious now that Luke means me no harm at all, but for what this means for my entire life. Everything feels upside down and inside out right now, including me.

"What if I say yes?" I finally say.

"Then I would say that I want to help you get there, help you find your family."

Curiosity piques within me. "Have you visited it?"

Luke shakes his head. "I have a feeling that if I try to reach it, I will drown. I don't think the city is intended for human visitation."

"Can anyone else see it?"

He shrugs. "There's no whiff of it on the local gossip vine, so as far as I know, no. I tried to show it to Holly, Christine and Alejandro once, but the storm got too dangerous on the jetty — we couldn't make it out here."

"Do they believe you about it?"

"Christine and Holly do; Alejandro thought it was just one of my old boyhood pranks, and I've let him believe that. It's easier than trying to convince him of the truth."

My brow furrows. "Does the Sunny Sea Bistro mermaid logo have anything to do with this?"

Luke laughs. "No, Sunny just loves mermaids." He slants me a sidelong glance. "The mythical kind, of course."

I smile. "Of course." Breathing a sigh, I stretch my legs out on the rock. "Is this what you and Christine were talking about yesterday? Mermaid City?"

"Yes." His face creases in apology. "I wouldn't have shared anything with Christine about you or us if I could help it, at least not in these early days. But she saw us all tangled up in the kitchen and then it was interrogation time for me. And I can tell you in all seriousness — *nothing* gets by Christine. She knew I was holding back on something, so I told her my thoughts about you. And I'm sorry if that betrayed trust with you."

"It's okay. I know how close you and Christine are, and I'm also aware of her gift of piercing through all levels of deception or withholding."

Even though Luke and I are having this very candid conversation, I still haven't stated outright that I'm a mermaid. And he hasn't asked me directly either.

Luke's gaze shifts out to sea. "I've wondered all these years why I am seemingly the only person who can see the city." He turns to me. "But then you arrived. From the first night I saw you walking along the beach with wet hair and damp clothes I knew that you were…"

"Different?" I offer.

"Special. And it was like all of these puzzle pieces started to fit together. I understand now why I'm the only one who can see it — it's for you. I've been waiting to show you all these years, and I never even knew it until recently."

We watch each other for a few quiet moments, almost as though seeing one another in an entirely new light. Which essentially, we are.

"The Mermaid City portal is only open for a couple of hours once per year?" I ask.

Luke nods. "Yes, as far as I know."

"So what does that mean for us?" If I can access the city with Luke, then it likely means that I will leave to start a new life with beings who are like me, and possibly even family.

A veil of bleakness darkens his eyes. "That part I don't really understand; it's confusing as hell. A part of me didn't want to tell you, because I think you might actually be warming up to using Poppy Bay as a home base when you're not traveling. And a part of me had started to hope, wonder if maybe we could be together, more than just a casual thing."

During their conversation at the barbecue, Christine told him he needed to tell me because it was the right thing to do, though I completely understand his inner conflict.

"I feel the same way about us," I say, lifting his hand to my lips for a tender kiss. "And you're right, I have been considering Poppy Bay as a new home base."

Leaving for Mermaid City would change all of that, and there's no guarantee that I would be gone for only one year until the portal reopens. So much can change in a year anyway, for Luke and me and *us*.

I lean into Luke, and he wraps his arm around my shoulder. Being with him here and now feels so good and right. But what if there really is an underwater city filled with other merpeople like me? And what if, in just a few days, I can access that city?

"Do you think the city will appear again this year?" I ask, peering out at the vast ocean before us.

Luke matches my seaward gaze. "I'm certain it will."

Chapter 13

Later in the evening, Luke meets me at Wild Rose Cottage for a walk along the beach.

When he sees the towel draped over my shoulders, his brow creases in question. "Are you going for a swim?"

I shine a beatific smile up at him. "Something like that."

When we left the jetty earlier today, I still hadn't come out and confirmed to Luke that I'm a mermaid. And he still hadn't asked me directly. So I've decided that tonight I'm going to show him, and if he goes running for the sand dunes at the sight of my large iridescent tail then I'll just have to find a way to mend my broken heart.

I don't think he will though, not after what he shared at the jetty, including his feelings for me. But still, I am feeling a little bit nervous.

It's one thing to see merfolk swimming far in the depths of the ocean, and another thing entirely to be up close and personal with one.

Luke and I hold hands as we walk along the dark beach, and when we get to the boulders at the north end of the bay, I begin to climb one of the rocks that juts out into the water.

Luke follows me up; we reach the top and find a flat area to sit on. We watch the waves and the sleeping seals bobbing serenely in the water.

Taking Luke's hand in mine, I turn to look at him. "I want to show you something."

His lips curve in a half-smile. "Okay."

I stand on the boulder and step slightly behind him to remove my clothes and set them near the towel. Without a word, I step beside Luke and dive into the inky water. The biting cold hits my human form, and some of the seals awaken at my entrance into their space, though most of them remain in a peaceful slumber.

I shift into my mermaid form, knowing that it must be difficult for Luke to really see me in all of the darkness.

My tail is shimmering in the water, and with its illumination, I know that Luke now has a brighter view of me. With my large mermaid eyes that can see clearly in the dark, I watch Luke as he observes me with an unreadable expression.

I give a gentle flap of my tail on the surface of the water to give him a better view of it, and his lips melt into a wide grin.

"You're beautiful." His voice is quiet and filled with awe. "Like a dream."

I exhale in pure relief, and proceed to glide around the boulder-shielded part of the bay while Luke watches me with shining affection suffusing his eyes.

"I'm going to get out now," I tell him after a few minutes of swimming. "Can you bring my clothes and towel to the shore? It's easier to exit that way than trying to climb the rock from the water."

Luke grabs the towel and clothes, and meets me at the part of the shore that is concealed by the boulders.

I leave the water in my naked human form, and Luke says, "My eyes are closed. Promise."

I approach and see that his eyes are indeed squeezed shut.

"Such a gentleman," I say with a laugh, tugging the towel out of his grasp. "Especially considering you've already seen me au naturel." Dressing quickly in my leggings and sweater, I tell him, "You can open your eyes now."

He opens his eyes and peers at me; there's a blended expression of desire, affection and intrigue on his face.

"Are you going to tell Christine?" I ask, feeling the slightest thread of anxiety tug across my chest. It's fine for Luke and my dad to know, but I'm not really sure how comfortable I feel about anyone else being privy to this information just yet.

"I won't tell Christine, or anyone, anything you don't want them to know." His tone is sincere and serious, and I believe him, wholeheartedly.

"Thank you. If we can just keep it between us for now, that would be great." Then with a laugh, I say, "Though Christine is likely to suss it out by just looking at one of us, so I don't know how secret the secret will remain."

"Very true," he replies with a grin. "I'll do my best though."

"That's good enough for me." I wrap my arm around his waist; he immediately responds by draping his arm over my shoulder, and we walk back towards my cottage.

We reach the driveway, and I pause to peer up at him. "Are you okay with this? With me?"

Luke's lips press together in a flat line, and he says nothing for an eternal moment. Little quivers of doubt begin to permeate my body, and my breathing halts on an inhale.

Finally, he says, "Lullaby, you're a mermaid. It's who you are, and I love it. I understand that a great level of discretion and responsibility comes with this knowledge, but I want you to know that I'm all in, in whatever ways I can be considering the circumstances."

With a start, I realize that he's the first of us to actually say it aloud—that I'm a mermaid. And he said it as though it's the most normal thing in the world, not like I'm something to be studied or feared, but that it's just who I am. My heart squeezes for the man standing before me, a remarkable man who I may very well be falling in love with.

"Thank you." My voice is laced with layers of emotion. "For everything."

"Luke?" A voice calls out from one of the walking trails.

Luke and I both turn towards the voice, and a couple holding hands walks up to us from the direction of Trillium Cottage.

Luke's expression lightens as he says, "Diego. How are you getting settled in?" He draws the young man into a hug, then embraces Diego's partner.

"The cottage is great," Diego replies with a smile. "We just got back from Main Street, for dinner and a couple of drinks."

Luke introduces the couple to me as Diego—Alejandro's nephew—and his wife Sierra.

"We're on our honeymoon," Sierra explains, her cheeks flushed with the glow that comes with being newly married to someone you deeply love.

"Congratulations on your marriage," I say. "How are you enjoying Poppy Bay so far?"

Sierra looks up at Diego with open admiration. "We love it."

Diego mirrors the look of pure ardor and adds, "Sierra wants to come back every year for our anniversary."

Luke smiles warmly at the couple. "You know you're always welcome to stay here."

Sierra breaks her gaze from Diego to beam at Luke. "Thank you, Luke."

Diego runs his fingers through his long black hair. "Yeah, we really appreciate it." A slight frown forms on his face. "We've been having some issues getting the fire started in the cottage—would you be able to take a look at it? I know it's late; I'm sorry to throw this on you at this hour."

"It's no problem at all," Luke says. "I'll meet you over there to take a look at it."

"Thanks, man. You're the best." Diego waves, and he and Sierra walk to Trillium Cottage.

I look up at Luke with a grin. "Is Trillium Cottage reserved for friends and family?"

He chuckles. "Something like that. Wild Rose and Trillium are somewhat separate from the rest of the property, and closer to my house so I generally put personal acquaintances in either one of them."

"That makes sense." I lift onto my toes to kiss his cheek. "Thank you again for everything today."

Luke links his fingers with mine, brushing his lips across my wrist. "You're welcome, and thank you for showing me more of your beautiful self." He thumbs to Trillium Cottage. "I have to go take a look at the fireplace now, but I would like to take you somewhere in the morning. It will be in the very early hours, before sunrise. Are you up for it?"

"An adventure with you?" My heart soars at the invitation. "*Yes*. Where are we going?"

Luke lays a kiss on my lips and says with a twinkle of amusement in his eyes, "You'll find out tomorrow."

"Fine," I drawl with a feigned touch of resignation. "I'll see you in the wee hours of the morning."

Chapter 14

The sky is still twinkling with stars when Luke and I get into his truck before dawn the next day.

Luke takes a local route south, one that is flanked by towering redwoods. The trees are like silent sentinels in the nightscape, guarding the magical secrets of the California coast.

I quietly observe Luke's profile while he drives; even in the shadows of this hour his presence is like a sun—warm and golden and powerful.

"What are you thinking?" he asks without turning to look at me, though there is a smile etching his profile.

With a quiet chuckle, I shift my attention to the road. "I'm thinking that I like how you can sense me watching you."

There are no other cars on the road this early in the day, and there's a feeling of peace suffusing the dark landscape around us. It's a little too cold at the moment to have the windows down, but even still I can hear the waves of the bay, and just under my skin I can feel the deep pulse of the ocean, like a fathomless echo of my own heartbeat.

Luke turns onto another road and drives slowly under a large sign suspended over the street. It appears that we have arrived at Poppy Bay Marina.

Sitting up straight in my seat, I ask, "Are we going out on a boat?" I can barely contain my excitement; next to swimming, boating is one of my favorite activities.

He clicks a small remote on his keychain to open the security gate. "Yes."

The parking lot is empty as Luke parks and we exit the truck, with the cool night air seeping into my jacket. Taking my hand in his, Luke guides me along the marina slips, where boats in various styles and sizes are docked.

Stopping at a slip with a sleek speedboat secured to it, he steps onto the vessel and extends his hand to me. I step aboard and take a seat next to the pilot's chair, which appears to be raised to accommodate Luke's height.

"Is this your boat?" I ask as he unties the vessel and drives out of the marina.

He smiles. "Yes." He appears to be perfectly in his element, navigating us into the open waters of the bay with skilled ease. Tilting his head at me, he asks, "What does it feel like when you shift into your mermaid form?"

I give a little shrug, closing my eyes to enjoy the crisp sea air on my face while feeling renewed appreciation for Luke's aversion to small talk. "It feels really natural, like my whole body just blinks into that form."

"Do you know any other merpeople?"

Opening my eyes, I shake my head. "I've spent my entire adult life traveling the world and searching for other merfolk, but I haven't met any yet."

Luke glances at me, his expression one of compassion. "It sounds like that would take a toll on a person after a while—all that searching and never actually finding kindred beings."

I give a low laugh. "Yeah, that's what my time here in Poppy Bay was supposed to be about—taking a break from all of that." My eyes shine with affection. "Instead I met you, and you revealed Mermaid City to me."

Luke's profile softens into a tender smile. He navigates the boat out of the bay and steers south, with the night sky expanding vast and endless high above us. There's a tinge of muted gray just at the horizon, so the sun will soon be rising.

Luke drops anchor just past the bay, and turns on a few lights that shine over the water. Taking my hand in his, he peers out into the illuminated darkness.

We watch the water in silence, anticipation buzzing throughout my veins, until a collection of silver-gray fins begins to cut through the waves.

I give a little squeal of glee. "*Dolphins.*"

Luke turns to me with a grin. "There's a large pod of them usually here this time of year; I thought you might like to swim with them."

Reaching up, I wrap my arms around his neck and smack a loud kiss on his cheek. "This is so sweet of you, thank you." Next to whales, dolphins are the closest thing I have to family in the sea, and I love spending time in their bubbly and buoyant energy.

Without a moment's hesitation, I strip off my clothes and dive into the ocean, shifting into my mermaid form before hitting the icy water. The dolphins click their greetings at me with cheerful friendliness, and I merge seamlessly with their pod.

I spend the next hour frolicking in the water with the dolphins — playing, splashing, zipping through the waves and chattering with them like the best of friends.

Luke watches us the entire time, laughing and appearing to have just as much fun from his place on the boat. As the first rays of dawn begin to appear in the sky, I pause for a moment to simply bob in the water and observe him, with my heart expanding out across the entire ocean.

Not only did Luke immediately accept me for who I truly am, he has also encouraged me to be myself by bringing me out here to play with the dolphins. The love that is growing within me for him feels so profound, and also a little overwhelming in its greatness.

"I'm ready to get out," I tell him, feeling as bright and happy as the vibrant sunrise colors.

Luke opens a large towel and holds it out for me. With a wave to the dolphins, I shift back into my human form and climb the ladder that extends up the side of the boat. Turning to Luke, I see that his gaze is pointedly fixed on the horizon.

Taking the towel from his grasp, I say softly, "I appreciate your continued propriety, Luke. But you don't have to look away each time we do this."

Luke clears his throat, his eyes still focused on the far distance. "Based on our time together in the shower, I'm sure you're aware of the effect your body has on my body... So I'm just trying to not spend our ride back to the marina with a cumbersome and distracting erection."

I give a little laugh. "Ah, I understand."

He points towards the bay. "Plus we're about to have company."

My attention shifts to the bay, where several small fishing boats are headed in our direction. I understand now why Luke brought us out here so early—not only does night swimming offer greater concealment in general, but it also ensures an absence of other boaters.

Luke takes the pilot's chair while I tug on my socks and pants. He's facing the steering wheel, with his back to me. Wrapping the towel around my bare chest, I walk to him and gently swivel his chair to face me.

I place myself between his knees and say, "Thank you for this, it was perfect."

His eyes flit down to my towel and back up to my face. "You're welcome."

Opening the towel, I wrap my arms around his neck and bring my lips to his, pressing my bare breasts to his jacket in the process. His breath hitches at the connection, and I deepen the kiss.

When we part, I peer over Luke's shoulder at the ocean, where several large seabirds are bobbing on the waves.

Still watching the birds, I say, "Luke?"

"Yes?" I can feel that he's watching me intently, but I keep my eyes averted to the water.

I inhale a deep, steadying breath. "I want to tell you something."

His fingers wrap around my waist, with his large hands radiating heat across my cold skin. "Okay."

Finally, I look at him; he's watching me with blueberry-blue eyes that are incandescent in the early morning sunshine.

"I'm falling in love with you." My voice is soft, raw and somewhat foreign to my own ears.

One corner of his mouth curves into a half-smile. "I know." Lifting a hand from my waist, he tucks a strand of damp hair behind my ear. "I feel the same way about you."

I breathe a sigh of relief, then my lips immediately clamp into a tight line of distress.

Luke's eyes soften into understanding. "I also know the 'but', Lullaby. It's Mermaid City. There's a new life there for you to discover and explore, with beings who are like you."

My lips slowly uncurl from the grip of my teeth and I nod. He gets it—he always does. It's one of the reasons I love him so much.

I lay a hand on his chest, feeling the steady, strong beat of his heart beneath my palm. "What are we going to do?"

He leans in to kiss my lower lip with delicate tenderness. "We'll enjoy the time we have together now." He continues to explore my mouth with soft, gentle kisses, the slow deliberateness of his lips igniting hot desire low in my belly.

Curling my fingers into his hair, I press him closer to my body, feeling an acute need for the physical connection.

Luke's lips move from my mouth down my neck and across my collarbone. His head dips lower to my breasts, and taking a taut nipple in his mouth, he clamps his teeth gently on it and tugs.

A fractured gasp escapes me, and I wedge my hips closer to his groin. So much for preventing a "cumbersome and distracting" erection.

His mouth shifts to my other breast, licking the salt off of my skin and taking that nipple between his teeth. He suckles while I rake my nails through his hair, directing him to continue with raspy breaths of encouragement.

The sound of another motorboat draws nearer, and Luke lifts his head.

"Rascal," he mutters, drawing the towel around my chest with smooth adeptness.

"Hmm?" I'm so dizzy and disoriented that I scarcely register what he's saying. "Rascal?"

"The other boater. I know him."

Turning towards the approaching vessel, I see that it is getting ever closer rather swiftly. I quickly dip low to tug on my bra and shirt, and begin drying my hair with the towel just as the boat pulls up alongside us.

An elder man waves to us and calls out, "Good morning, Luke! Catch anything good yet?" The deep lines on the man's friendly face tell me he's spent many a morning on these open waters.

"Morning, Rascal," Luke says. Sliding me side-eye, he continues, "Nothing yet but a few nibbles."

I dip my head to conceal the fit of giggles rippling out of me, and Luke waves to Rascal before driving us away from his boat. After docking at the marina, we devour gigantic breakfast burritos from a food truck in the parking lot then drive back to town.

"What's going on?" I ask Luke when we reach Main Street, which is heavily congested with traffic. Vehicles are merging onto the thoroughfare from all directions, and even the sidewalks have increased crowds of pedestrians.

"It's the visitors for the meteor shower," he replies, deftly navigating both the vehicular and foot traffic.

"I've never seen it so busy on Main Street."

There's a kind of collective energetic buzzing around the town now, like a massive hive of bees converging on Poppy Bay.

Taking a moment to open my mermaid intuition, I check if there are any other merpeople in town, but I don't get any pings back.

When we arrive at Luke's house, he gets a call from his property management company regarding multiple special requests from new guests at several of his rentals.

"I have to head out again to take care of these requests." He gives me a swift kiss at the trailhead of my cottage. "I may be tied up for the next couple of days, managing guest needs and all the other little things that come up this time of year."

I steal one more kiss from him and reply, "I will keep myself busy in the meantime and see you whenever it works for you." I take the trail back to Wild Rose Cottage, with a little piece of my heart already lamenting his absence.

Chapter 15

Luke wasn't kidding about getting tied up with work stuff.

I didn't see him at all yesterday, and we only briefly saw each other this morning, with just enough time to exchange swift kisses and a quick conversation about Mermaid City before he had to take off for work again.

I was at least able to use the Luke-free time yesterday to check in with my assistant, who has been managing most of my business affairs during my sabbatical, and to prepare her for a possible extended absence. I also called my dad.

After letting him know about Mermaid City, and how it could potentially take me out of human engagements for at least a year, he offered to come to Poppy Bay and be with me before I departed.

I considered Dad's offer and finally declined, telling him that I wasn't at all confident things would work out with Mermaid City as a long-term destination.

In the brief moments Luke and I spoke this morning, we outlined a Mermaid City visitation strategy, where ideally I would just visit the city and get a feel for it during the couple of hours the portal is open. This way I won't have to commit to a full year or longer there, which I'm not even sure is possible.

Are the denizens of Mermaid City welcoming to outsiders, even ones who are like them? What if they do welcome me, and I find out the city is just one small part of a magical ocean world, one I want to spend the rest of my life exploring.

With all of these variables swirling around in a nebulous cloud of possibility, it's hard to be certain of anything at the moment.

I let my dad know I would keep him updated on Mermaid City, and we ended the call with him expressing excitement and deep love for me. A part of me wishes I could take him—and Luke—on this underwater scouting mission. Dad would love it, and Luke, well, I want to experience all new things with him.

But contrary to popular belief, I'm not actually able to give humans the ability to breathe underwater, at least not as far as I'm aware. And maybe Dad and Luke could use scuba gear, but if Luke's sense is that Mermaid City is not intended for human visitation then I want to honor that. Plus, I don't want to place them in any unnecessary danger. So this first visit at least, will be a solo journey.

Now it's the day before the meteor shower, and the town of Poppy Bay has become even more saturated with amateur astronomers and enthusiastic stargazers. And though I am enjoying their exuberant energy from afar, I've been mostly keeping a low profile to avoid the crowds.

However, after feeling a bit of cabin fever between yesterday and today, I've decided to leave the cottage to have lunch at Sunny Sea Bistro.

The bistro is brimming with diners when I enter; there's even a line of guests waiting to be seated stretching out the door. When I search the dining counter, I'm relieved to see one free stool left, in the far corner of the restaurant.

As I approach the coveted stool, I notice that Christine is sitting in the chair next to it, munching on a sandwich that's about as tall as a skyscraper. She's wearing her sheriff's uniform, and her chair is pushed out quite a bit to accommodate her belly. When she sees me approaching she waves me over.

"Are you here for lunch?" she asks. "If so, you can have this seat next to me. It's the last one available."

"Thanks," I say gratefully, pulling out the stool and sitting. "What's in your sandwich? It looks amazing."

"This is the turkey avocado club," she says around bites. "It's delicious."

A server approaches me from behind the counter, and I order the club sandwich and a glass of water.

Shifting on my stool, I survey the packed restaurant for a few moments, musing on how busy it is.

Noticing my contemplative expression, Christine asks, "How are you faring with the crowds?"

The server brings out my water, and I lift the glass to take a sip. "Crowds aren't really my favorite, but I'm handling them okay. Is everyone behaving so far?"

"We've had a couple of incidents, but nothing too severe." Perhaps Christine doesn't enjoy talking about work on her lunch break, because she changes the subject fairly quickly. "Luke mentioned you run a travel lifestyle business, and Holly said she loves your books."

"Yes, the business is called Lullaby's Travels; it's fun work for the most part."

Christine finishes the first half of her sandwich before responding. "Where's your favorite place to visit?"

My lips purse in consideration. "There are so many, but I really love the stark beauty of Norway, the lushness of Costa Rica and the mystical feel of Ireland."

After asking the server if he can pack up the other half of her sandwich, Christine turns to me with her penetrating sheriff's gaze. "Do you have a favorite of them all?"

I cast her a wry smile. "You probably wouldn't believe me if I told you."

She lifts a brow, and I give a little snort of laughter, remembering her bionic ability for detecting truths, and lies.

"Here. My favorite place is here. Well, California in general," I clarify. "There's everything here: ocean, desert, mountains. I love the people in this state, and the easy access to Portland, Seattle and Vancouver."

She nods a few times. "Do you think you'll ever be able to settle in one place?"

Ah. I see what's happening here. This is not just a friendly chat about my career, though I shouldn't have assumed it would be with Christine. What she's really doing is interviewing me to gauge my worthiness for Luke.

"No," I answer honestly, noting the mildly positive appraisal in Christine's sharp expression, which I imagine is mostly due to my frankness. "I believe there is a part of me that will always be seeking the next adventure, but I do want a home that I can spend time at more often than not, and have the travel be a bonus, rather than my primary activity."

Her eyelids partially lower as she regards me for a few moments, almost as though she's patiently waiting for me to say something incriminating. Finally, she offers, "Luke also likes to travel."

Holy moly, is she actually getting on board with Luke and me as a couple?

Immediately dispelling that fanciful notion, she adds, "But you'll be gone soon anyway, so that really doesn't matter."

I'm not sure if she means I'll be gone to Mermaid City, or off on another travel adventure, but I don't ask her to elaborate. I feel confident that Luke has kept true to his word and not told her anything about me being a mermaid. She may already sense it intuitively, but I'm not going to feed her any information that will confirm it, at least not today.

The server brings Christine's leftovers, telling her that Sunny—who has been slammed in the kitchen with Alejandro—added a couple of snickerdoodle cookies for dessert.

Thanking the server, Christine stands from her stool. "The crowds will thin after the meteor shower," she says to me, "but it really is a fun event to watch. I think you'll enjoy it." With a small nod, she exits the restaurant.

I watch her leave, wondering if I passed or failed the interview.

Chapter 16

The night is all darkness speckled with stars as I make my way to the north end of the bay where the large boulders are clustered.

There's no bright moon illuminating the sky, so it's perfect viewing conditions for the meteor shower.

Luke is at the boulders waiting for me; I got caught up in a phone call with my dad and let Luke know I'd meet him at the rocks. Dad shared some information he found on underwater dwellings thought to be related to merpeople, in the hopes that it may help with my visit to Mermaid City.

"I saved you a spot," Luke says when I climb the highest boulder to where he is sitting. He chose a spot that looks like a natural stone bench, and he has a blanket wrapped around his shoulders. Opening the blanket, he invites me to sit next to him.

I gently push apart his knees and place myself between them instead.

"Is it okay if I sit here?" I ask, turning around to meet his eyes. Even in the darkness, I can see his pupils dilating.

Wrapping the blanket around both of us and kissing the back of my head, he murmurs, "More than okay."

I recline into the solid warmth of his chest, inhaling the sun-kissed forest scent of him. "Will Christine and her family be here tonight?"

"Christine is working tonight, and she'll likely be busy. Omari and the kids are at the swimming beach. Most people go there—it's where the jellyfish tend to cluster most densely since the water there is calmer."

That explains the very few people scattered on the boulders and beach in this area, though to me the rough waves crashing into the rocks sound like the proverbial music to my ears.

"I'm glad you chose this spot," I say, burrowing further into the blanket with a contented sigh. "I like the privacy."

His mouth slowly sweeps across the back of my neck, just below the ends of my chin-length hair. "I'm glad you chose *this* spot. Easy access to kiss you."

I turn my head to meet his lips in a soft kiss. When we part, Luke points up at the sky.

"It's starting," he says.

A few brilliant shooting stars streak down the sky, and I squeak with delight. "I see them!"

Luke wraps his arms around my chest. "Keep an eye on the water as well."

My attention shifts to the water, and I gasp. It appears as though stars have literally fallen from the sky and landed in the water. Phosphorescent dots of blue, green, white and lavender are lighting up the depths, like the heavenly bodies in the sky have found a new home in the bay.

"The *jellyfish*." My voice is laced with wonder at the incredibly magical display taking place before my eyes.

Glittering fireballs are streaming down from the sky, in a way I've never seen before in my life. The jellyfish are brightening one by one, filling the bay with a symphony of incandescent color. The combined beauty of it all steals my breath, and I lean back into Luke, observing the extraordinary phenomenon with quiet awe.

"Are you enjoying it?" Luke asks in a low voice, his breath a swirling wisp just behind my ear.

"Immensely. It's fantastic." I run my hands up his legs and linger near the zipper of his jeans, idly toying with the seam there.

We watch the luminous display in the sky and the sea, while I stroke along the fly of Luke's pants. The more I caress him, the more desire unfurls within me, until my attention is more focused on touching him than viewing the spectacular nature show.

The front of his jeans is stiff with arousal, and I run my hand up and down his length, feeling his staggered exhalations just near my neck.

Luke's fingers trace down my hooded sweatshirt and to my jeans, where he mirrors the movement of my hand. Sucking in a breath, I widen my legs to give him better access. His free hand reaches up to my face, gently turning my chin to face him. Our lips meet in a deep kiss, while his other hand continues to stroke up and down the seam of my pants.

My hands trail down his legs and to the button of my pants. I undo the button and, drawing the zipper down, guide his hand into my underwear.

His fingers slowly slide down, until he arrives at my damp heat. My breath quickens as his middle finger languorously circles my ultra-sensitive nub, and it takes all of my willpower to not cry out at the intimate touch.

How many nights have I envisioned Luke touching me in this way? Too many.

And now it's really happening and *oh God*, it's so very much better than my fantasies.

Two of his fingers slide down farther, curving up and into me. My hips rock back against him while he explores my body, sliding in and out to circle the bud that is pulsing wildly for his touch.

Luke continues in this way, stroking and circling with fingers that are criminally skillful, until I'm panting and cresting like the waves crashing all around us. There's light exploding across my vision, and I don't know if it's the shooting stars, the jellyfish, or my own essence radiating out for miles beyond my body.

I grab Luke's free hand and press it over my mouth, clamping my teeth onto his palm to prevent myself from howling into the night.

Heaving a few deep breaths, I collapse into his arms, limp and feeling as though my soul just shattered and reformed in an entirely new configuration.

Luke trails light kisses across my temple, where little beads of perspiration have gathered despite the chill of the night.

"I would love for my mouth to be there," he says in his low-timbre voice near my ear. "I want to taste you, Lullaby."

I turn to face him and take his mouth in a possessive kiss, swiping my tongue across his with ardent need. I break the kiss and meet his hooded gaze.

"I need you, now," I whisper to him, breathless and quivering for more.

Luke says nothing. Instead, he stands and holds the blanket around me while I zip up my jeans. We climb down the boulder and stride straight to his house, leaving the stars to burn down from the sky into the sea.

Chapter 17

I'm in Luke's kitchen boiling water for peppermint tea early the next morning, and there's a smile on my face that has been glowing there since last night, with the only exception being when my countenance is contorting in orgasmic bliss.

So that would be multiple exceptions then.

I think Luke's sexual appetite surpasses even mine; this is a first for any of my romantic partners, though it is nice to finally be with someone who can keep up with me in this way.

My shower fantasy with him finally came to fruition last night, and all I can really say about that is that the reality of having sex with Luke in the shower is far more delicious and toe-curling than anything I could possibly imagine.

The water in the kettle begins to boil, and I grab two mugs down from the cabinet. Luke emerges from the hallway, wearing only a pair of boxer shorts. His hair is tousled in an indescribably titillating way, and his lean form looks positively archangelic in the scattered rays of early morning sunlight.

I'm wearing a loose tee and cotton panties, which Luke runs his hands up and down as soon as he reaches me.

"Good morning," I say after giving him a long, lingering kiss.

"Good morning." Luke's voice is sexy-gravelly and rough, much like the dark stubble covering his jawline.

I pluck two peppermint tea bags from the rack on the counter, set one into each of the mugs and pour boiling water into the cups.

Standing close behind me, Luke draws my hair aside and brings his mouth to the nape of my neck. I place the kettle back on its heating element and close my eyes to enjoy his lips on my skin. He trails slow kisses over my neck until my fingers grip the counter and a little moan departs me.

Running his palms down my arms, he guides one of my hands to my panties, gently sliding it to where liquid heat is already pooling.

"Touch yourself, please," he politely instructs near my ear.

He doesn't have to tell me twice.

I slip my fingers into my underwear and across my silky wet opening, while Luke's hands reach under my shirt and up to my breasts.

He pinches my nipples, gently and with little twists that leave me panting for more.

"Pinch them harder," I command with a gasp. And because we're being so polite, I add, "*Please.*"

His fingers compress tighter, creating a delicious sort of pain that lies solidly in the realm of pleasure. My fingers slide over my nub, rubbing it with increasing pressure.

The sound of the front door opening reaches us, and Christine calls out, "Luke?"

"Damn it all to hell," he mutters into my hair, tugging my shirt back down to my waist. "I'll meet you in the bedroom."

I scurry off quickly and vanish into his bedroom. With a massive giggle blended with a sigh, I flop across his bed belly-down and grab one of the high fantasy novels on his nightstand. I open the paperback to a page near the middle to occupy my time while Luke is with Christine.

Only a few minutes pass before Luke enters the bedroom, and I tilt my head up at him with my lips pressed together to prevent myself from laughing.

"That was interesting," I say, waving my legs leisurely through the air.

Luke groans. "That was excruciating. I told Christine she needs to knock first and wait for me to answer the door, new rules."

"Did she know that I'm here?"

He tilts his head, and a wry smile curls on his lips.

I laugh, turning my attention back to the book. "Of course she did."

He settles behind me on the bed, with his knees on each side of my hips. "I'm very open about my feelings for you, Lullaby. So I'm glad Christine knows you're here. The only reason I asked you to come into the bedroom is because I wanted to finish my conversation with her *very* quickly and get back to this." Lifting my shirt, he trails his lips down my spine and to the hem of my panties.

My breath falters, but I continue reading.

He traces his lips over my underwear, then clamps his teeth onto the left side of my bottom.

"Ouch," I cry out, but I don't shift away.

Luke plants a kiss where his teeth just were. "You like it."

A little giggle courses out of me. "I do like it."

Lifting my hips so that I'm on my knees, he asks, "Are you enjoying the book?" His fingers begin to caress over the hot, damp crease in my panties.

"Yes, immensely." My voice sounds somewhat bizarre to my ears, like a whisper-whimper combined with a moan.

"What part are you at?" His voice is thick, low, almost purring as his fingers slide back and forth with languid strokes.

"Um..." The words are beginning to blur on the page; I really can't focus on anything but his incredibly adept fingers at the moment. So I answer his question with a question. "The part where the elves are fighting the bad guys to save their kingdom?"

Luke draws my panties down to my knees and begins to circle at my slick entrance. Slow, leisurely circles that have me gasping with shallow breaths.

"Am I distracting you?" he asks softly.

"Yes," I breathe, turning a page in the book even though I have no idea what I just read.

"Do you want me to stop?" Slow circles all around, now one finger sliding into me.

"*No.*"

"What do you want, Lullaby?" he asks in a gentle, coaxing voice.

111

I press my hips back, plunging his finger deeper into me. *"I want you inside me."*

His finger slides out, and I can hear him removing his boxers behind me. He grips his large hands onto my hips, with the tip of his hard length nestled firmly at my entrance.

I close the book with a moan, tossing it onto the floor.

He sinks deep into me.

Chapter 18

Luke and I have been living in a love bubble for the past couple of days, and tonight we're expecting the Mermaid City portal-opening storm to hit the shores of Poppy Bay.

We've only emerged from our cubby of mutual adoration once to video call my dad. I introduced Dad to Luke, and we sorted out some of the personal and business affairs they would take care of in the event of my extended absence.

The way that Luke has stepped in to help with everything doesn't really surprise me because that's the kind of person he is, though I'm also somewhat astounded, mainly because neither of us has any idea how long my visit to Mermaid City will last, or if I will even return.

Will I explore the city for just a couple of hours during the storm? Stay for one year? Longer?

Even with the uncertainty hovering on the fringes of our awareness, Luke has still been a steady and unwavering presence. My appreciation for him goes far beyond words, and it feels as though my heart has cracked wide open, with expansive love rippling throughout my body in pretty pastel colors.

After tonight though, there's no guarantee that Luke and I will still be an 'us'. And that somber thought has threads of apprehension coiling darkly around all of my heart's light.

I'm really trying to let all of the anxiety go until we actually arrive at the jetty tonight, and I get to explore the city. Then I'll have a better idea of what comes next.

We've decided to have lunch at Sunny Sea Bistro today; Luke's fridge is starting to look a little sparse.

I'm wearing a cornflower blue sundress—a cute one with a row of tiny yellow flowers stitched around the empire waist—and the feel of the toasty sun on my shoulders and legs feels heavenly. Luke is casual in a heather gray tee and jeans, and even with our vast height difference, I'd still say that we make a very lovely couple.

We enter the bistro; it's busy inside, though not at the same level it was on my previous visit before the meteor shower. Luke and I veer towards the dining counter, and an elder couple waves him over to their table.

"They're regular guests at the cottages," he tells me, planting a kiss on the top of my head. "I'll be right back."

I take a seat at the counter, and Sunny greets me with a bright smile. Today, the barrettes fastened in his silver-white hair are two adorable dolphins.

"What are you having today, dear?" he asks.

I glance over at Luke talking to the couple at their table. "I'm actually here with Luke; I'll wait for him to order."

My gaze lingers on Luke, who is laughing with the couple and appears to be entirely in his element conversing with them. He must sense my observation, because his eyes suddenly lift to meet mine.

His lips spread into a slow smile, and my heart melts into a puddle at my feet. He is so handsome and kind and just absolutely perfect.

Sunny gives an unintelligible little murmur from behind the counter and I turn to look at him, clamping my lips to conceal a wide—and likely ridiculously smitten—grin.

Sunny's hazel eyes twinkle with delight as he says, "I already know what Luke will be having: the grilled chicken on brioche with sweet potato fries."

"Oh, okay." Pressing my fingers to my cheeks, which feel hot and are likely suffused with pink splotches, I quickly peruse the menu and order the Greek salad wrap.

Luke arrives at the counter when Sunny is setting glasses of water down for us, and he and Luke exchange friendly banter while we wait for the food to arrive. Once it does, Sunny leaves us to check in with the other diners, stopping by occasionally to see how we're doing.

With all of the vigorous activity Luke and I have been enjoying recently, it seems that both of our appetites are beyond ravenous. I eat every last morsel of my wrap and even help myself to some of Luke's fries, while he devours his sandwich in just a couple of bites.

As we're getting up to leave, Alejandro emerges from the kitchen for a quick greeting. He doesn't say anything about Luke's hand entwined in mine, but I do notice him and Sunny exchanging sage smiles just before we turn and exit the bistro.

"That was delicious," I tell Luke when we get back into his truck. "Just what I needed."

Luke starts the engine and shines a satisfied smile at me. "Same for me."

He begins the drive back to his house, and I quietly watch his hands on the steering wheel while he navigates the streets. Those large hands have brought me to multiple levels of pleasure in recent days, and just looking at them is igniting an altogether different kind of hunger within me.

Casually, I place my hand on his leg and run it down and up his thigh in slow, smooth movements. I do this a few times until shifting to trace the seam of his jeans and discovering that he is already stiff with arousal. When we reach a stop sign, he casts me a brief sidelong look, and I smile ever so sweetly at him.

Leaning down, I open the button of his jeans, tug down the zipper and draw his hard length out of his boxers. There's a drop of dew beading at the tip, and I swipe it away with one silky caress of my tongue.

"Don't mind me," I murmur, licking the head of him slowly. "You can just focus on driving safely."

Luke grunts but says nothing, his breath catching with every pass of my tongue.

I lick him with languorous strokes, down his shaft and back up to the tip. My lips part wide, and I take him into my mouth until his head taps the back of my throat and I can take in no more.

A low growl emerges from Luke's chest. "*Lullaby.*"

Lifting my head, I look up at him with half-lidded eyes. "Do you want me to stop?" I ask softly.

"God please, *no*." His eyes never leave the road, though when I angle my head I notice the whites of his knuckles as he grips the steering wheel.

I dip my head and continue savoring him—down deep in my throat and back up to his tip.

We must arrive at his house, because Luke throws the truck into park and grips my shoulders.

"Come up here, Lullaby," he commands in a low voice, pulling me up and spreading my thighs to sit astride his lap. His eyes are as dark as a midnight storm.

"Hello," I breathe, wiping my mouth and grazing my damp heat over his erection.

"You didn't wear underwear today," he murmurs, lifting my dress up to my waist. "Perfect."

He strokes his fingers over my wet opening; a wanton moan flows out of me, and he guides me down onto him. I'm so ready I take him in like a channel of liquid silk.

With my hands gripping the headrest, I immediately start riding him with a savage rhythm, my hips slamming into him with feral abandon.

One of his hands reaches up to grasp the back of my head, and he pulls me close to take my mouth in a possessive kiss. His other hand reaches down between us, with his thumb running circles over my aching nub.

We're so beautifully in sync, even in our frenzied movements, and I rock into him until every cell in my body is fragmenting in climax.

"*I'm coming*," I cry out, digging my nails into the seat fabric and arching my back like I'm surfacing from the depths of the sea.

There's one, two rough lifts of Luke's hips as he thrusts deeply into me, followed by a guttural groan. "*I am too.*"

We cling to each other as electric shockwaves pulse between our bodies, until finally I collapse in his arms.

Luke draws me back to kiss my nose, cheeks and forehead.

"That was incredible," he murmurs, running his thumb along my damp hairline.

"Indeed," I agree, laying a few kisses on the salty-sweet skin of his neck.

We dot kisses onto each other until our breathing normalizes, then Luke shifts so that I can extract myself from his lap. He reaches into the backseat and passes me a clean beach towel so I can tidy myself up.

Grabbing my purse, I open the passenger door and plant my feet on the side step, but I don't actually get out of the vehicle.

Luke exits from the driver's side and walks around to me, his eyes creasing in mild concern.

"Is everything alright?" he asks, entwining his fingers in mine.

"Yes." I give a little laugh. "My legs are shaking, so I need a minute." I tug him between my knees, leaning close to kiss his lips.

When we part, he tucks a strand of hair behind my ear. "Take as much time as you need."

I peer up into his heavenly blue eyes, a whirlpool of emotions swirling within me.

"I wish the storm wasn't coming tonight," I blurt, both surprised and relieved to be stating it aloud. "I'm really excited about Mermaid City, I am. But this, us…" I trail off and run my fingers through his chestnut hair, which is tousled and slightly damp from our spirited exertion.

He touches his forehead to mine. "I feel the same way."

What neither of us says is that the love between us is so new, and it may never have the opportunity to flourish into something profoundly greater.

With a silent sigh, I step down from the truck and walk with Luke into his house.

Chapter 19

"The storm comes every year at sunset?" I ask Luke, watching violet and orange light striate the sky.

We've just finished dinner—after a trip to Main Street Market to replenish Luke's fridge—and we're now sitting on the rooftop sofa with a light blanket draped over our legs.

The sky looks calm now, though as soon as we sight the storm we're going to leave for the jetty.

Luke nods. "Every year since I first saw Mermaid City. We can head out now though, if you prefer."

I nestle into his side and lay my head on his shoulder. "Let's wait for the storm to start; I want to enjoy this with you now."

Luke places a gentle kiss on my hair, and we watch the sky's colors shift as the sun slowly descends into the bay.

Flickering starlight begins to appear in the twilight sky, and my lids flutter with fatigue. Outside of our sustained lovefest, most of the time Luke and I have spent together has been devoted to planning for my potential absence, and it's all finally caught up with me.

I try and keep my eyes open, but my body has other priorities and I soon fall asleep.

* * *

"Lullaby?" Luke awakens me with tender kisses sometime later.

My eyes drift open and I see him kneeling near me, watching me with infinite love in his gaze. Beyond him is a clear night sky scattered with glimmering stars.

"Is the storm starting?" I ask, my voice laden with sleep.

"No, I'm going to bring you inside." With one adept maneuver, he lifts me off the sofa and descends the stairs that lead into his house.

I nuzzle against his neck, inhaling his woodsy essence. "What time is it?"

"It's after midnight."

We enter his bedroom, and he lays me on the bed. I tug the covers over me, and Luke comes to lie by my side so we're facing each other.

Tracing my fingers along his jawline in the dark room, I ask, "Has the storm ever come this late before?"

Luke shakes his head. "No."

"Maybe it really won't come this year," I say softly, though I'm not entirely clear on how I feel about the notion—relieved, sad, hopeful, disappointed? It's a lot for my brain to process at the moment.

"Maybe." His voice is laced with the same kaleidoscope of emotions as mine.

121

I trail my fingers up his cheek and over his lips. "I love you, Luke. Whatever happens, or doesn't happen. I love you, always."

Luke brushes his lips across my mouth and touches his forehead to mine. "I love you too, Lullaby. Always."

My hands reach down to lift up his shirt, and we quietly undress one another in the darkness. Our lovemaking tonight is luxuriantly slow and sweet, like we have ribbons of eternal time together.

When we are both sated and spent, I curl up into Luke's arms and we fall asleep in a deep embrace.

* * *

I'm awakened sometime later by Luke again.

"Lullaby, the storm has started." After a few kisses on my temple, he shifts out of bed and starts pulling on his jeans.

I sit up in bed, immediately hearing the wind and rain outside the house. The powerful gusts screeching against the window sound fierce, with the battering rain seeming equally harsh.

I stand and begin to get dressed. "How long has the storm been going on for?"

Luke flips on the bedroom light and grabs his backpack. "A while, I think. I just awoke to it a few minutes ago, but I think we've slept through a lot of it."

I inhale a deep breath, tugging on my jacket and shoes.

The storm is here.

It's time for me to explore Mermaid City and determine if it will be my new home.

This is really happening.

A spell of dizziness ripples through me, and I sink onto the bed.

Luke is immediately at the bed, kneeling in front of me with great concern in his eyes. Taking my fingers in his hands and kissing the tips of them, he asks, "What is it, love?"

"I'm feeling overwhelmed. This is all really exciting, but it's also…a lot."

Luke's hands release my fingers to run up and down my legs in slow, tender movements. His breath is coming deep and steady, and I mirror his breathing to calm myself.

"It's alright," he tells me in a low, soothing voice. "You can do this; you were meant for it. Okay?"

I nod, inhaling a few more deep breaths before standing from the bed. "Okay." I zip up my jacket, with a swell of determination expanding within me. "I'm ready."

We leave the house, with both of us getting soaked by the rain on the short walk to Luke's truck. The storm is raging all around us, and wild waves are crashing roughly into the nearby shore.

Luke drives north towards the jetty; the rain is pelting hard onto the windshield, and heavy gusts of wind are billowing all around the vehicle.

After only a couple of miles, Luke slows on the road, turning on the high beam headlights. There appears to be something obstructing the lanes, and as Luke pulls up closer a fallen tree becomes visible.

The tree is completely blocking the road, making it impassable for us.

Chapter 20

"I know another way," Luke says, shifting his vehicle into reverse and turning back in the direction of Poppy Bay.

He turns onto another road, a narrow and winding one that is flanked by dense redwoods. The wind is wailing through the trees like a tortured ghost, and with the rain there's barely any visibility in front of us.

Luke keeps his eyes on the road the entire time, while a well of anxiety begins to flood my body.

He must sense my distress, because one of his hands reaches over to briefly squeeze mine.

"I will get you there on time," he says. "I promise."

I nod, aware that he can't see me doing so since he's still focused on driving safely. I don't think that's really what I'm feeling anxious about though.

A part of me is afraid that he *will* get me there on time. And what if Mermaid City is just another disappointment? What if it's only a sea mirage, an illusion and nothing more? Or what if it is real and I leave Luke—and my human life—for something entirely new and unknown.

Even though I generally thrive on newness and adventure, this particular adventure feels a little too permanent. With our slow driving progress, and the length of time the storm has already been active, it's highly unlikely that I will be able to just visit the city as initially planned.

We spill out of the winding road of redwoods onto a main route with the coast on our left. Luke turns into the jetty parking lot, though the stormy darkness is obscuring any view of the rocky structure.

He parks the truck, grabs his backpack, and we both step out into the storm. The trees in the cove are swaying wildly in the wind, and the cold rain is pricking mercilessly through my layers of clothing.

Taking a firm grip on my hand, Luke guides me out to the jetty; he has a look of raw determination on his face that is apparent even in the soppy chaos.

Harsh winds are shoving at us from all angles as we make our way onto the rocks, with waves crashing ferociously into both sides of the structure.

But still Luke continues.

"If we get knocked into the water, hang onto me!" I shout at Luke through the wind. I will be able to navigate the turbulent water in my mermaid form, and get him safely to shore if needed.

Luke nods, and we trudge forward until it suddenly feels as though we're stepping through a gossamer curtain of energy.

On the other side is utter peace, and complete calm.

Luke turns to me with a wide grin of satisfaction. His hair is beyond mussed and his clothes are soaked, but his eyes are alight with pure joy.

"We made it," he says, tossing his backpack onto a large rock. He draws me to him for a hug, and I wrap my arms around his lean waist and squeeze hard. I am so incredibly thankful for this man I can't even put it into words.

I release the embrace and lift onto my toes to kiss his lips. "Thank you," I tell him when we part, "for getting us here safely, and for experiencing this with me."

"You're welcome," he replies with a generous smile. He points towards the ocean, just over my shoulder. "Look."

I shift my attention to the water, which is peaceful with mild waves lapping onto the jetty rocks.

Deep beneath the surface of the water is a sparkling emerald city.

Mermaid City.

I step to the edge of the jetty and peer down into the water. It really is there—an expansive city with buildings glimmering in various shades of green, from pale mint to deep hunter. And swimming around the buildings are merpeople.

My people.

Just as Luke described, their iridescent tails are swishing like trails of starlight, and there appear to be many of them as the city seems quite vast.

I look up at Luke, my eyes wide and pooling with tears. "*Luke.*" It's all I can say at the moment.

He clasps his hand in mine and kisses my wrist. "It's here for you, Lullaby."

I inhale a sharp breath and turn back towards the sea. A part of me just wants to sit on the rocks and watch the city, immersing in the complete awe and wonder of it all. But the storm is already starting to abate.

Just around our curtain of calm I can see it — the winds are dying down and the rain is diminishing to a drizzle. Even the trees in the cove look less like palm trees in a hurricane and more like the sturdy redwoods they are.

I have to go to the city. And based on the abating storm, it appears as though I have to go *now*.

Turning back to Luke, I say, "The storm is ebbing."

His eyes are filled with compassion and love. "I know. You have to go, and not just for a quick visit."

I nod, swallowing down the lump of emotion forming in my throat. "Can you call my dad? I didn't have time when we were leaving, and I'm sure there's no signal out here."

Luke takes his phone out of the backpack and confirms the lack of service. "I'll call him as soon as I get back."

"Please tell him... Tell him how much I love him, and that I'll see him when I return." *If* I return.

"I will." He reaches into the backpack again and draws out a bikini top. Not his favorite black one, but a more modest purple one.

I give a little laugh when I see it. We packed the top because I wasn't sure what the nudity etiquette would be in Mermaid City, so I wanted to be prepared just in case.

I take off my jacket, shirt and bra, and put the bikini top on. I also strip my jeans off, leaving my underwear on for now.

Lifting onto my toes, I wrap my arms around Luke's neck and place a deep kiss on his lips.

"I love you always," I say.

He brushes a few tears from my cheeks. "I love you too, always."

He wraps his arms around my waist, and I burrow into his neck, inhaling his earthy essence for one final moment.

Something begins to vibrate deep within my bones, and my breath stutters on an exhale.

It's a mermaid call.

The notes shimmer throughout my entire body, similar to how the whale call did on Luke's terrace, but this call feels vastly different.

It feels *familiar*.

I draw back from the embrace and peer down at the water. The notes come again—they're high, light and crystalline, similar to my own call.

My head snaps up to Luke. "*It's my parents*. They're down there, waiting for me. I can feel their call vibrating within me."

Luke's eyes widen, and a massive smile melts across his face. His eyes glisten with unshed tears as he says, "That's incredible; it's time for you to go home and be with your family."

"You're my family too." It took me standing on the precipice of connecting with my biological parents to realize that, but it's true. Luke *is* my family, and I will never forget that. Or him. No matter what happens in Mermaid City, which is just beginning to fade in the ocean.

I tug down my panties and lift up to hug Luke with infinite love pulsing in my heart.

"Take care," he murmurs into my hair, drawing back to lay a tender kiss on my lips.

"I will."

I don't ask him to wait for me; it wouldn't be fair to do so. I have no idea how long I'll be gone for, or what will change in both of our lives once I'm in Mermaid City.

I run my fingers through his damp chestnut hair, then turn and dive into the water, swiftly shifting into my mermaid form.

I surface for a final wave at my beautiful love, and with a flap of my tail, I dive deep and swim home to Mermaid City.

Chapter 21

Throughout my travels, I've learned that each place I visit has its own unique pulse; it's a special energy that makes it unlike anywhere else in the world.

England for example, has a deep, steady pulse that speaks of ancient wisdom and enchanted lands. Most of the Caribbean has a sexy, sultry pulse that feels like making love on a white sand beach. Mermaid City's energy feels like an ongoing summer solstice celebration: light, joyful, playful.

When I first arrived at Mermaid City, both of my parents were waiting for me at the entrance, along with many other merfolk who all greeted me enthusiastically and warmly, as though I really was being welcomed home.

The group were as diverse as humans—in all shapes and sizes—though all of them tended to have either a purple or greenish tint to their varied skin tones.

I noticed that many of the merpeople with breasts had small shells covering their areolas, though the shells appeared to be purely an accessory, as many others were swimming around with their breasts unadorned. No one batted an eye at my purple bikini top, and as a newcomer I felt immensely grateful for the lack of comment on my chosen attire.

After the initial welcome, my parents guided me through the underwater metropolis, pointing out various landmarks and greeting other denizens.

Most of the city was decorated with brightly colored ribbons and baskets overflowing with a rainbow of sea flowers. When I asked my parents if there was some sort of celebration underway, they informed me that merpeople are always celebrating something: life, love, unions, seasonal cycles and even just the beauty of a new day. They also confirmed what Luke suspected—the city is not intended for human visitation.

My parents, Finniden and Marielle, are a very attractive couple with features that are strikingly similar to my own. My father, Finniden, is broad and tall, though I do have his black hair and olive skin with greenish hue. My mother Marielle and I share a curvy-petite frame and gold-flecked brown eyes.

They are really lovely merfolk, and during our initial conversation at their home, they shared with me the reason I was adopted by humans.

My parents—who are very tapped into divine knowing and soul wisdom—explained that I had a pre-birth intention to inspire humans with my magical mermaid perspective, which I've done primarily through my work with Lullaby's Travels.

Surprisingly, my parents also knew all about my travel lifestyle business; they gleaned this knowledge via magical merfolk mirrors that can view the human world. They assured me though, that the mirrors only highlighted certain aspects of my life and not anything that would be deemed an invasion of my privacy.

When I asked them about the lack of other merpeople in the human realm, Marielle and Finniden told me that many merfolk have chosen to remain in their underwater cities. This is so they can support the continued thriving of Earth's oceans in a more direct manner. They did also say that there are still some merpeople living in the human realm, just not as many as there once was.

Overall, the experience was everything I ever could have hoped it would be—I got answers to my most paramount questions, my parents were kind and loving, and Mermaid City was a delight to spend time in.

But...it wasn't Poppy Bay.

Poppy Bay's unique pulse is magic, mysticism, beauty and wonder. It's golden threads of sunlight woven with silvery threads of moonlight. But mostly, the special energy of Poppy Bay feels to me, like home.

Which is why I'm here now, one year after leaving for Mermaid City. It's early morning and I've just stepped onto the beach from the depths of the sea.

Digging my toes into the soft sand, I close my eyes and inhale a deep breath, relishing the fresh air and warm sun on my skin. After so much time spent in the ocean realm, it feels surreal—in a good way—to be standing on solid ground again.

I open my eyes and begin walking over the sand dunes towards Luke's house, tugging nervously on the straps of the backpack my parents gifted me for the trip back here.

So much can change in a year, and I have no idea what—or who—is going to greet me when I arrive at Luke's home. A new dog, or perhaps a new lover?

I reach his house and pause just at the end of the driveway, squinting into the expansive windows. There's no movement within the living room, and there are no summer-fun sounds coming from the backyard either.

I should just walk up to the front door and knock; I can always make an excuse and leave if someone other than Luke answers.

Breathing in a couple of deep, steadying breaths, I resolve to do just that, when the front door opens and Luke steps out.

Chapter 22

Luke is wearing a white tee and jeans, with his chestnut hair curling in damp waves like he just got out of the shower.

He locks the front door and turns to walk towards his truck, spotting me standing at the end of the driveway. There's an inscrutable look within his blueberry-blue eyes that's remarkably similar to Christine's penetrating stare.

I tug on my backpack straps again, feeling like the new kid in a new school—unsure if the locals will welcome me.

The silence between us stretches for eternal moments, until finally Luke's lips melt into a wide smile.

That's all I need to see.

With a quick intake of breath, I run to Luke and jump right into his open arms.

He lifts me off my feet and presses me to him for a tight embrace.

"You're back." He's studying my face with searching eyes, almost as though he's not sure I'm really here.

"I'm back," I breathe, quickly blinking away the tears forming in my eyes. It feels so good to be in his arms again.

"How was your adventure in Mermaid City?"

I nuzzle into his neck to inhale his heavenly sunlit forest scent. "It was an adventure."

Luke sets me down and assesses my attire with one swift sweep of his eyes. "I think this may be my new favorite outfit on you; the black bikini is now in second place."

I look down at my ensemble with a chuckle. "I got it at a shop in Emminoa, which is the real name of Mermaid City. They have a great fondness for sparkly things in Emminoa, though I do feel somewhat like a dominatrix with a penchant for glitter."

The outfit is similar to a bathing suit, in a royal blue material that's covered in silver glitter. There are thin strips of sparkly fabric running across my chest and stomach, teeny tiny shorts and minuscule triangles barely covering my nipples. All of the strips of fabric are held together with gleaming silver rings.

"I now love that shop in Emminoa," Luke says with a grin. His eyes lift from my clothing to my face, and his expression grows pensive. "I was at the jetty last night; I didn't know if you would come, but I wanted to be there just in case. I waited most of the night, but there was no storm."

I reach up to stroke the dark stubble on his beautiful jawline. "That's so sweet of you; I had a feeling you would be there." I glance at the beach and back at Luke. "The portal has moved. It's shifted farther out to sea, which is why it's taken me so long to get here."

"I'm glad you made it here safely. Your dad asked for you to call him if you made it back."

135

"I will call him very soon, thank you for letting me know. How have you been? It's been a whole year since we last saw each other."

Luke rakes a hand through his damp hair. "I've been good, spending a lot of time with my new nephew and Christine's other children. Holly is doing her study abroad program; she's in Spain at the moment."

"That's great to hear, really great." I shuffle my feet on the driveway as a mild awkwardness settles between us. Now that the initial greeting has passed, it feels as though we're just getting acquainted with one another.

Luke's eyes sweep the ground and back up to meet mine. "So, the portal has closed then?"

I nod. "It has for now, though my understanding is that new portals will be opening more frequently between the human realm and underwater realm in the coming months. I don't know the details of it all, but there are supposed to be big changes underway, for both of our worlds."

Luke curls his hand around the back of his neck, with uncertainty—and questions—flitting throughout his eyes. "That's great, Lullaby. It sounds really exciting for you."

"Luke," I say softly, clasping his free hand in mine. "I want to be here, in Poppy Bay. I mean, I still want to travel for work and fun, but I want to be with *you*…if that's still an option?"

His blue eyes gleam in the sunshine—with relief, elation, love. "Thank you, for not drawing this part of the conversation out, and for getting straight to the heart of the matter." He pulls me in for a deep kiss. "And yes, that is still very much an option. I've thought about you every day for the past year."

"I've missed you dearly," I say. "And every day I was gone I thought about how much fun it would have been to experience the underwater world with you by my side."

His lips twist in thought. "So, no impossibly handsome merman swept you off your tail while you were there?"

I draw his hand up and brush my lips across his knuckles. "Not even close."

He lifts a brow, a hint of a smile on his lips. "Mer*maid*?"

With a giggle, I say, "No love, there's only you."

"That's good to hear." His voice is the low timbre that I've missed so much, and my heart squeezes at being able to interact with him in this playful way again. "Will you tell me about Emminoa? Is there more than the one city?"

"Yes, there's an entire underwater world and I will tell you all about it later. But first, my parents would like to meet you—are you up for it?"

Luke peers over my shoulder, his eyes searching the beach. "I'd love to meet them; are they here now?"

"Kind of." Digging into my backpack, I pull out a hand mirror. It's an opalescent metal one with tiny peach shells embedded into it. In place of the reflecting glass is a plate that looks a little like liquid mercury swirling with blue light.

I hold the mirror up so both Luke and I can see into it, and essentially video call my parents. Their lovely faces appear in the mirror, and Luke's eyes widen in surprise, though his expression quickly shifts to his classic warm and welcoming one.

"Luke," I say, motioning to the mirror. "These are my biological parents—Marielle and Finniden." My parents wave enthusiastically, and I continue speaking, running my hand down Luke's arm. "This is my…" My words trail off as I fumble to find the right one. Is he my friend, lover, human? None of those labels feel quite right, and I peer up at Luke for clarification.

He offers me a tender smile, then turns to the mirror. "I'm Luke. It's a pleasure to meet you, Marielle and Finniden."

I throw a grateful smile at Luke, and he engages my parents in friendly conversation as though it's the most normal thing in the world to be speaking to merpeople through a mirror portal of communication.

We complete the conversation with my parents, who offer to visit us when the new portals are open on a regular basis. I tuck the mirror into my backpack and turn to Luke, my lips creasing into a small frown.

"Even though I've spoken to my parents about you at great length, I still didn't know how to introduce you. I'm sorry about that."

"There's nothing to apologize for." Luke entwines his fingers in mine. "I've been thinking about something along those lines as well." He pauses, his expression shifting into reminiscence. "Do you remember the first night we met, when you said you just may have to marry me?"

I give a short laugh. "Yes, I'm pretty sure I was delirious with fatigue at the time."

He places little pecks on the tips of my fingers. "That kind of stuck with me anyway. And I've been thinking, that if it feels right for you, that maybe I can be your husband."

My eyes widen and my breath catches in my throat. "Really?" For the second time today, tears are beginning to

138

pool at my eyes, but this time I don't try and blink them away.

Luke's eyes gleam with lucid ardor. "Yes. I want to travel the world with you, watch sunsets together, sit in a field of wildflowers and take you to swim with dolphins. I love you, with a depth that rivals the ocean's, and I want to explore and experience all of life with you." His free hand lifts to tuck a strand of damp hair behind my ear. "So Lullaby, my beautiful mermaid, will you marry me?"

"*Yes*," I say without hesitation, my heart expanding out for miles around me. "I love you too, and I absolutely want to marry you."

"Good." With a deeply satisfied smile, he lifts me up into his arms and kisses me ever so deeply.

I wrap my legs around his waist and curl my fingers around the nape of his neck, desire flowering low in my belly.

"I would love a shower and change of clothes," I murmur, trailing my hand down his shoulder and to his chest.

He runs his fingers slowly along my bare thighs. "All of your belongings from Wild Rose Cottage are here, so there's plenty to choose from."

"Thank you." I squeeze my legs around his waist, pressing my hips closer to his lean form. "This outfit was really complicated to get into, so I may need some help getting out of it."

His pupils expand into wide black saucers. "I volunteer myself for that task." With my legs still wrapped around his waist, he turns to swiftly unlock the front door. He

139

walks us over the threshold, and anticipation shimmers throughout my entire body.

A wonderful adventure is just beginning here in Poppy Bay, one where Luke and I explore new landscapes of love, together.

About the Author

Tina Marie Christensen has been writing magical stories for as long as she's been reading them, and she loves featuring beautiful settings in her books.

She currently lives in California, where she enjoys laughing with her husband, napping with her cats and exploring the enchanting landscapes of the Golden State.

Join Tina Marie for magical musings and author updates at: tinamariechristensen.com

Also by Tina Marie:

Dream
Mystical romance novella that beautifully blends fantastical dreams and waking reality.

Crescent Moon Falls
Magical romance novella set in an enchanting manor house in the wilds of Northern California.

Adia: City of Light
Atlantean adventure romance set in Lake Tahoe in the majestic Sierra Nevada mountain range.

all titles available on amazon

Made in the USA
Middletown, DE
29 October 2023

41508105R00090